ELIOR:
PRINCE OF FAE

Joshuan Rivera Jiménez

Archway Publishing books may be ordered through booksellers or by contacting:

Archway Publishing
1663 Liberty Drive
Bloomington, IN 47403
www.archwaypublishing.com
844-669-3957

ISBN: 978-1-6657-0204-1 (sc)
ISBN: 978-1-6657-0205-8 (e)

Library of Congress Control Number: 2021901753

Print information available on the last page.

Archway Publishing rev. date: 02/17/2021

PROLOGUE

The nervous excitement before a momentous occasion always leaves you wondering whether you should smile brighter or hold your hands out, for your heart could fall out of your mouth at any moment.

My travel companions, Grayson and Willow, and I had been on separate journeys for months before we banded together in search of the portal to the fae realm.

And today, we finally knew how to find it and leave the human realm.

We were brought together out of necessity. However, you take what you can get when you are being hunted.

"Jules, can you procure more apples? I fear these plums will not last longer than two more days," Willow asks with concern in her voice. She is fixated on what fruits to bring as an offering to the fae, thinking it will affect their decision whether to let a group of changelings in or not.

The fae are known to take in any and all nonhumans who request admittance. Since the Great War, humans have been on the warpath with anything that threatens their power. And, I guess being only part-human and descendants of fae qualify us as a threat.

"I am positive the fae will not care how long the fruit we bring them will last," I tell Willow as I get ready to fetch some apples. "Knowing the fae, they likely have any fruit they desire in bounty."

"We can't be overprepared, though," Grayson says under his breath, loud enough for me to hear. His nerves have manifested in a sour attitude and an odd overprotection of Willow, whom he befriended a few weeks ago after arriving in South Carolina.

We've been hitchhiking by the side of the road for weeks, making our way up north. Grayson received word from a relative in New York that a group of our kind is requesting asylum in the fae realm during next week's full moon.

I call it luck that I ran into Grayson in Georgia. He claims it was the beginning of "the Age of Aquarius," and that nothing is a coincidence under this cosmic change. He seems to believe in many things, whereas I don't even know if I believe in myself—or his saving grace.

Because the government entered into another war, our kind is sought after. We have two choices when they track us down—join, or die.

I'm not sure I believe how great the fae realm is, but what choice do I have? So, up north, I continue, with two flower children obsessed with fruits.

"We can catch a bus straight to New York in Washington," Grayson adds. He's right, of course. We're in Virginia right now, so that shouldn't take us too long. "The longer we stay on the road, the bigger a target we become. It's too suspicious for three people to be hitchhiking together and have no one ask any questions."

He can sometimes be so logical. Yet at other times, he speculates how extraterrestrials infiltrated Harvey Glatman's mind and made him commit horrible murders.

"Then we're going to need to find apples soon, Jules," Willow instructs once more.

"All right, all right, I'll look for apples," I relent. I think I saw a gas station or a store across the woods a few minutes ago while we were walking.

The establishment, which indeed is a gas station, sells apples. I check my pockets and find I only have about twenty dollars left to my name. I can't afford to be wasting money on apples when we still need to buy tickets for a bus.

"Good afternoon, sir," I say with a big smile upon entering the gas station store. "Would you happen to know if there's an orchard nearby? My daughter is insistent that we get her a Virginia apple just like George Washington."

The attendant is awestruck, but I'm used to that when I look like I do right now—tall, voluptuous, with long blonde hair. I always turn boys' heads.

"Good afternoon, ma'am," he stutters. "I'm afraid the nearest orchard is not for another forty miles west of here. We do have some apples here for sale. How many do you need?"

"I reckon a basket full would do," I say, flashing the biggest smile I can and playing dumb.

"That's no problem at all. I can ring you up here and take it to your car myself," he says.

Wrong answer. I look around and see that the only other customer at the station has finished pumping gas and is on his way out. The attendant is going to figure out I came by foot.

Before he can look outside, I walk toward him, maintaining eye contact.

"That would be … splendid," I say in a sultry voice that never fails me. He's entranced with me. This should be quick.

"I can … I can … help with the …" he stammers, as I unbutton my dress to expose some cleavage.

Once I'm close enough, I grab the lanyard on his neck. He's all smiles until I yank it downward with full force slamming his head against the counter and knocking him out cold. I grab the basket of apples and rush over to Willow and Grayson.

My travel companions don't question from where I got the apples or the basket.

Appeased with the damn apples, Willow stops fidgeting, which in turn calms down Grayson. The rest of the trip to Washington is largely uneventful. At night we take turns keeping watch, and every few miles some kind stranger stops to give us a ride. Even during the bus ride to New York, we each keep an eye out while the other two sleep.

Once we arrive, we head directly to Central Park where Grayson's great-uncle said to meet on the night of the full moon. We still must find the group.

At the park, there's a broad mix of people. Families, individuals, couples … they all look different from each other. Grayson has only seen his uncle in pictures. This park is not small—it spans for miles. We could walk in circles all day and all night and still miss the group completely.

We're wasting time just standing around with fruit in our hands.

"What's the big plan now, Gray?" I ask with more attitude than intended.

"We must go deep into the woods," he confidently says as he grabs Willow by the hand and leaves me to carry the basket of apples.

Sunset is approaching, and we're wandering the woods without a single soul in sight. Well, that's not entirely true. Every so often we get close to the roads and see other people. It's our cue that we have strayed off.

Hours pass and exhaustion starts to kick in. Willow is adamant about not eating the offering, so we settle for some of the bounty that's about to spoil. As we sit in a small clearing, I can't help noticing how her hair turns brighter as the day becomes darker. It's a small detail that I don't think she notices herself. But it probably speaks to the horrors she endured as a child and gives her a way to keep the light on during dark times.

"Good evening, ladies and gentleman," a voice says behind me. I turn to find a stout white-haired man with an impressive mustache. "Are you lost?"

Crap. He must be the park police, a ranger, or whatever they're called.

Grayson stands up with some doubt in his eyes. "We're looking to change our course. Go somewhere new, in fact."

The stout man draws a smile and begins to transform right before our eyes. His limbs extend, his straight white hair turns to wavy dark locks, and his face completely transforms to that of a Black woman who simply says, "Come with me, children. You're among family now."

They found us, thank the heavens. As we follow the tall woman through the woods, I can't contain my excitement. I see Willow and Grayson giggle at each other. The woman instructs us to keep quiet until we reach the group. We're finally leaving persecution.

We arrive at a larger clearing, now under the full moon. There must be at least fifty changelings present.

The organizer of the group is talking, explaining what's about to happen, and keeps referring to an old book he's holding. My mind is torn in different places. I'm relieved to be leaving this realm. Yet I can't help but think back to my daughter. She's not a changeling and won't be persecuted like me. Still I can't fathom how my leaving her with no explanation will make her feel. She'll probably resent me for her entire life. But at least this way we'll both be alive. Who knows? Maybe if things calm down I can come back and explain everything to her.

Here and there, I catch some of what the organizer is saying; something about tenets and offerings. I guess Willow was right to get the apples after all. We're instructed that we need to make a request as a group.

Sure enough, everyone starts holding hands so we can all be connected. I place the basket on the floor to free both limbs. Willow is holding my hand on her left and Grayson to her right. With my left hand, I hold a skinny man's trembling hand. His hands are clammy and shaking. I tighten my grip in an effort to provide some stability.

We haven't spoken to anyone here. As I look around I see shifting faces—people growing taller or changing hair color like Willow. You can feel desperation in the air. We would not be here if we had any other choice. I can't help but think about what each of us must have left behind to be here tonight. It doesn't make the fact that I left my child behind any easier. However, it does provide some solace that I am not alone in making sacrifices. Misery loves company, I guess.

I can't fully hear the organizer with the book who is doing some sort of chant in English and kneeling. I don't understand why he sounds like a preacher. Maybe the fae like it? Just as they would like a random basket of apples from Virginia?

Without warning I see a ring of golden fire materialize in the sky not too far above the organizer's head.

With all the light shining in my direction, I can only make out two large figures with insect-like wings that glow bright enough for my eyes to delineate. One figure holds a wooden staff like that of a cartoon wizard—what I imagine Gandalf the Gray would carry. Willow grasps my hand so hard that she might break it. I look and I see tears streaming down her face. Grayson is also smiling. It's the first time I've seen him truly beam. We're finally safe.

The man next to me releases my hand. I look up to see that the light and the two angel-like figures are gone. Grayson, Willow, and I knock over our basket of apples as we rush over to where the organizer stands.

"The king denied us entry," the organizer says flatly still on his knees.

My entire body feels numb. Everything is silent. I see Willow collapse in Grayson's arms as catches her amid his own screaming. We're going to die.

My only thought is of my daughter.

PART I

CHAPTER 1

Awakening

I wake up on the ground. Some kids in the park think I'm dead, so they come over to marvel at the dead guy with pink hair. The sun is disorienting, the heat is unbearable, and the smell is nauseating. Only one thing is certain—I'm in the human realm.

Think back. Think back. All I remember before waking up is seeing my dad pointing at me with his staff and everything transitioning from blinding light to darkness.

This is ridiculous. I'm alone in the human realm with a nagging feeling that I'm supposed to be with someone right now. My heart starts to beat faster and faster, and I catch myself breathing through my mouth, almost panting. No, I can't do this now.

Balance yourself, Elior. Assess yourself and your surroundings.

I'm relatively well, aside from a massive headache. I don't really remember why I'm wearing human attire, complete with blue jeans, a black T-shirt, and sneakers—something doesn't feel right.

Human children are around. My heart drops. My hands frantically reach for my back and shoulders. I'm unsure if the shock from the fright has debilitated my sense of touch. Are my wings showing?

Looking over my shoulder, I don't see them, but I feel them wrapped around my back and shoulders. I run my left hand over my right shoulder, slowly this time.

There you are, my friends.

This realm feels unconventionally warm. From my times here before, I remember the air feeling heavy or smelling of metal. Yet this time there's a tinge of decay assaulting my senses. Had my eyes been closed, I would've sworn I was walking through a wasteland.

I keep going back to that image of my dad, blasting me with light. Someone was behind me, but I can't remember why I was located between the two.

The human children keep staring. I muster my last bit of energy and say, "I am going to eat you up." I'm trying to sound playful, but it comes out groggy. The kids run back to the group of young parents sitting by the benches with their beverages. It's early morning. They stare back with the same confused expression I'm probably retaliating with. This is all making me feel afraid. I should just go home and figure out how I got here in the first place. I just need to cross the portal.

Um … Where is the portal?

I swear on the sun and the moon that I don't remember where it is.

Why can't I remember? How am I going to get home? Shit, shit, shit. I'm really stuck here.

I should stay put. I'm sure my father will send guards or a rescue team for me. I only hope they're able to find me in this polluted realm. Portals are usually secluded, and I can see the surrounding streets from any point of this park. My heart palpitations rise again. Better find a more appropriate place for a portal.

Human currency is one of the most annoying aspects of this realm: that and their disregard for nature. Hopefully, I can find a fruit trader who will show me kindness.

There seems to be a market located by the park's entrance. Perfect.

As I approach the market, I see a few fruit handlers.

"What is that, sir? Is that garment made of animal skin?" I ask the older gentleman behind a foldable table. His slim frame and white hair give his age range but not a pinpoint. It's hard to tell with humans. Their life spans are so much shorter than ours. The man's earnest smile and genuine excitement to be talking to someone gives me hope that the answer to my question is an unequivocal no.

"Yes, sir! Only the finest leather materials for my vests," he says cheerily. I almost feel bad for this human. It's as if he doesn't know any better. But then again, that's their self-serving nature—killing others and destroying things for their pleasure and gain.

"You, sir, are a disgrace. How dare you try to benefit from the macabre?"

"I'm sorry?"

"You killed a living being, skinned it, and now intend to trade its skin as if it were something that belonged to you to trade. That is disgraceful."

"You're with PETA, aren't you? I knew coming to Brooklyn that I would risk running into you hipster social warriors. But I wasn't expecting it would be the first person to talk to me."

Brooklyn. That's near New York City. A portal is there, that much I remember.

"I … um. Thank you? You seem like a nice gentleman, but you should reconsider your livelihood and your concept of life and respect."

I race out of the market area and out of the park altogether, then follow the sidewalk in search of a post. I find Weirfield Street and Wilson Avenue.

None of the posts point to New York. I'm going to need assistance if I'm going to get to the portal any time soon.

"I am Elior of Lempara, crown prince of fae folk, and I will return to my rightful realm," I whisper to myself in hopes of calming my nerves by setting a goal. "But first, I need some food."

CHAPTER 2

Collision

I still feel bad about yelling at that old man in the market. I know some humans do what they can to survive, given their circumstances. I'm walking aimlessly down the street and my stomach is rumbling. Humans have a bad habit of not having fruit trees around. That's always been the case with them. Can't coexist; they must dominate. There was a time when they coexisted with us and nature. But what I remember from my previous visits here, they have increasingly relied on their inventions and complex trading systems rather than the environment.

"Oh, a lemon tree!"

As I rush to the food shop across the street with the luscious lemon tree in its entrance garden, a terribly rude human nearly kills me with her metal contraption.

If I hadn't stopped, thrown my hands in the air, and balanced on my tiptoes, she would've knocked me over.

"You imbecile! You could have killed me," I shout at the blonde-haired woman in the leather jacket getting off her metal steed.

Motorcycle! I remember riding one, vaguely. Humans don't have wings like us, so they first depended on animals for their transportation. When that wasn't enough, they resorted to building their own mechanical ones. As horrid as motorcycles are, I find them fascinating—something I can never share with my family.

"Are you serious, dude! I swerved to not hit you, dumbass! You almost killed *me*!" she snaps back at me as she trots to the middle of the street where I'm still standing. "How can someone be so stupid to just run into the street like that?"

"First of all, how dare you raise your voice at me? You need to calm down and know your place."

"My *place*? You're talking down to me because I'm a wo"—her voice deepened—"man?" By the sentence's end, her hair seems shorter, and her features alter from soft to angular. Though she is still in the same black-and-white sundress, boots, and jacket.

"Wha—what was … what *are* you?"

"I'm the person who's going to kick your ass, pink."

It clicks in my mind. It is improbable but not impossible; much like their existence in the first place.

"You are being ridiculous. I care very little whether you are a man or a woman, but I do care that you are a changeling."

"A wha—"

The changeling can't finish her thought. She and I both hear a bullet whiz past us and shatter the window of the coffee shop with the lemon tree.

I turn around to face a group of three humans dressed

in black suits and sunglasses who are advancing toward us with weapons. I have no prior recollection of these people, but I don't think a rescue group shoots at you as a greeting.

"I am sorry, changeling. You mind if I take this?" I blurt as I run to the motorcycle.

As soon as I go, the three suited people run to a nearby black car, but the changeling chases after me. I get to the motorcycle before her, push it off its stand, and grip the throttle. I bolt off on the motorcycle in no particular direction, happy that my hands know what to do. I think I can evade them and hide out until I figure out another plan to get to New York's portal.

A swift escape will have to wait. The changeling's arm is abnormally stretched, grabbing the back of the bike and pulling herself toward me.

"Please let go! You are making me a target," I scream.

"You almost got me killed twice, and you want me to do you a favor and let you steal my bike?" she yells.

I briefly turn back to find an angry red-faced changeling trying to stabilize herself.

"I am terribly sorry to do this but—"

At the next crossroads, I take a sharp right turn.

"That's three times now you tried to kill me," she yells.

"I swear I am not! I am just trying to lose you—and yes, borrow your motorcycle."

"You know, you could've asked nicely, and I would've gotten you away from the murder trio following you," the changeling throws back at me as she inches closer in the seat.

Too late. Her arms wrap around my waist.

"Make a left at the next intersection," she barks.

I can still see the black car in my rearview mirror. When I glance again, the suited woman in the passenger seat pops out of the window with a weapon aimed at us.

"Turn!" the changeling shouts in a deep commanding voice, as she squeezes me tighter.

I follow her instruction, but as I do, the woman in the car fires her weapon, and a projectile hits a nearby vehicle. Startled, the motorcycle skids, so I release the throttle to find our balance again. But by that time, the murdering trio is already on our tails. Both the driver and the woman in the passenger seat are leaning out of their windows, aiming at us. This is it. Even with bad aim, one of them is bound to hit us.

"I will be damned if I die because of a pink-haired hipster," the changeling screams and jumps into a backflip, landing on the hood of the trio's car. Bewildered, the driver slams on the brakes, and the man in the backseat pops out to try to grab the changeling. Before he can start climbing on the roof, the changeling sprouts small bone spikes on her forearms and slams them into the car's windshield.

The changeling then stretches her legs, and in a few running steps, she is by my side again.

"Take a left here. I think there's a tunnel a few blocks from here, and we can get away from these people," she says.

As we ride off, I look back to see the trio getting out of the car—looking confused as to what the hell just happened.

CHAPTER 3

Introductions

We take fifteen turns before finally stopping by a wooded area with only a few houses surrounding it.

I turn off the motorcycle, and the changeling hops off as if I was suddenly the one covered in the spikes like she'd sprouted an hour earlier.

The changeling changes her appearance to a tall muscular male-presenting human with long brown hair tied in a knot. He now has a darker complexion than mine and sharp angular features. He is still in her leather jacket, but beneath it, is shirtless. I assume she is trying to intimidate me with a show of muscles, but the tight jeans just remind me of the way a tulip's skinny stem goes up to the wide base of its petals.

"All right, how are you going to pay me for my bike? And what the hell was that all about?" he asks in a booming chest voice.

The entire left side of the motorcycle is now scraped. The formerly good motorcycle now is fused with one from the pits of hell.

When I say nothing, he demands, "All right, what's your name? And where's your rich-boy credit card? We're going to an ATM."

Deep breath.

"My name is Elior, and I am not sure what type of card to which you are referring. Listen, I deeply apologize for damaging your motorcycle. I have no idea who those people are. I am just trying to get back home."

"Where's that accent from, Elior? And how do you *not* know who's trying to kill you?"

At this point, the changeling is a foot from me, looking downward and getting visibly exasperated with my answers to his questions.

"I know this must be incredibly frustrating for you, as it is especially so for me as well. I woke up this morning not knowing how I got here or what happened the night before. I was only looking for some food when I came across you, and those humans started chasing us."

Without fail, my frustration and confusion manifest themselves into tears streaming down my face. My skin immediately flushes and I'm embarrassed that I can't be anxious or frustrated without having waterworks all over my face.

The changeling will think I'm some crybaby. But maybe it's what I need for him to take pity on me and help.

"It sounds like you got hammered, pissed some people off, and passed out. Where is home?" the changeling relents.

"Uh, well, you see the issue with that is that it is not technically here …"

My gaze is directed groundward where some dying grass

is making its last attempt at flourishing—tattered, forgotten, and left to its own devices to survive.

"OK, no. We're not doing this. You nearly got me killed several times this morning. You are going to sit there and explain yourself and then take me to your obviously rich parents so they can pay for the repairs to my bike." The changeling is exasperated. If his unfriendly tone wasn't enough, he stretches himself a little taller through that last sentence.

The combination of sweat on my forehead and tears down my cheeks makes me feel disgusting. "Can we sit down somewhere first? I am still a little shaky from that chase, and I could really go for some fruit, changeling."

"Why do you keep calling me that?"

"Changeling? I assumed—given the display of your abilities back there and the lack of introduction."

The changeling comes down to my height.

"I … it's not like we met. You … you almost killed me. I go by Alex," he says absentmindedly. "How do you know about changelings? And come to think about it, why didn't you freak out when you saw me change?"

That's a funny reaction. "Interesting, I thought it would be more obvious to someone of your kind. Guess these human clothes do the trick." Alex's face seems perplexed. "All faes know about changelings. They are the closest species to ours. Our kinds have always been amicable to one another."

"Fae? As in fairies?" Alex lets out a loud mocking yell. "Hah! That is the stupidest thing I've heard in a while—and we were just chased by three people trying to kill us." His eyes widen, and jaw drops. "Oh my god, are you crazy? Is that why they were chasing us?"

"I am not sure about that. Those were humans chasing us. My father would have sent faes to bring me back. And no, I am not mad—I am fae. Why is that such a crazy thing? You are not human, either."

"Aren't you supposed to be small with wings and fairy dust?" Alex asks while clearly mocking me.

"There were smaller faes a long time ago. They could jump between realms very easily, without the need for a portal. It's why humans remember them better. I have no idea why you think that I should have dust," I explain.

"And, I do have my wings. Look." I lift my shirt and turn around enough for Alex to see my two bottom wings stuck onto my lower back.

It's sort of embarrassing not being able to fully connect with them. In any other circumstance, I'd be able to extend them and have a cool display for Alex. I know it's vain, but when new beings meet me, they're usually impressed by my larger wings over other fae, and it's odd to have a part of me incapacitated.

Mouth agape, Alex cocks his hip to the side and crosses her arms. "Well, I'll be damned. You are a fairy."

"Fae."

"Can you do magic?"

"Like what?"

"I don't know, levitate things or transform them or—wait, why didn't you fly away when those people came after you if you were so worried?"

A small tone of jealousy comes through from Alex. It

would be worrying if I wasn't so focused on getting some assistance.

"I … I cannot. I could not. I do not know what is wrong with me. I cannot extend my wings, and I do not feel any earthly connection to manage any energy."

It dawns on me that I have been pushing the sense of dread to the back of my mind. More than making it back home or not being able to extend my wings, I am worried that I don't feel nature.

The faes' connection to nature is inherently ours. It's not something you're taught; it's something that is a constant in your life since the moment we're born.

With two tear pools in my eyes and a clenched throat, I step toward Alex. "I know I just caused you a great amount of stress and unnecessary turmoil, but I am lost. I am trying to get home, and I do not know this realm all that well." My voice cracks. "I swear I do not know who those people chasing me were, and I am truly scared. I do not remember how I got here. All I know is that there is a portal in New York City, and that is my best hope of figuring all this out. Can you help me? I swear I will have my family pay for a new motorcycle and compensate you for your troubles."

Alex is visibly uncomfortable at my distress. "OK, fine. I need the money, and I'm pretty sure those people are not too happy with me after I destroyed their car. Luckily, I know how to go about undetected. However, before we go anywhere we need to hide that pink hair."

CHAPTER 4

Disguise

Alex and I wait outside a gymnasium for some time—at his direction. At this point, he looks rather unassuming. He has taken the form of a middle-aged brunette man of lighter complexion, wearing jeans and a light blue gingham button-down shirt.

"Can we simply go to an alley so I can change clothes?" I ask Alex, who seems to be waiting for something.

"Give it a minute," he says under his breath.

A tall, skinny woman in a yellow dress with shoulder-length brown hair walks out of the gymnasium. She is talking on her phone as she heads down some stairs to underground transportation.

"This is it," Alex says. But by the time my gaze travels from the woman to back to him, he has changed into the form of the woman we just saw.

I gather myself, grab my two shopping bags from the nearby shop we visited earlier, and follow Alex into the gymnasium.

At the front desk, a short girl with dreadlocks and a bright smile greets us.

"Oh, hello again, Dana! Did you forget something?" she asks Alex, looking puzzled and giving me a sidelong glance.

"Sort of," Alex replies in the woman's voice, with a smile on her face. "I ran into my stylist friend here when I walked out, and he just happened to have some pieces for me. Do you mind if we step into the locker room quickly so I can try them on?" Alex sounds cheerful and assured. It is incredible how she can transform outwardly and also adopt an entirely new character at the drop of a hat.

The front desk girl eyes the plastic bags in my hands and reluctantly agrees to let us through, under the stipulation that I am to wait outside the women's locker room for Alex—or Dana, in this case—to change.

As we walk upstairs, "Dana" changes her appearance to that of a younger muscular man in gray shorts and a black tank top.

"Why did you change again?" I whisper to Alex.

"Because we're here to disguise you, and to do that, we need to be in the same locker room without attracting too much attention."

When we enter the men's locker room, Alex empties the bags, opens the hair dye box, and begins mixing some liquids together that smell awful.

"What is that stuff, Alex? Wait, do I call you Alex?"

"I can easily change appearances and hide, but your pink hair is a dead giveaway. We're dying it brown. And, um … I guess you can call me Matt, for this form."

Alex—or Matt—isn't wrong about me needing to blend

in; we had received enough stares already. But it had also been an hour since the chase occurred, and no one was following us. I thought we could make it to New York with my pink hair intact. Albeit, I'm not sure where we would go in New York or what we'd do when we arrived … but one thing at a time.

The thought of being lost without memory hadn't crossed my mind in a while. Yet just like that, the image of my father pointing his staff at me before a flash of light hits me crosses my mind again.

"How may I be of assistance, Matt?"

After a half hour, Matt is disappointed and frustrated, as were the other gym-goers in the locker room who weren't pleased by the mess we were making by the sinks.

"How is it possible that not a single hair strand seems darker? This stuff is like tar," Matt bemoans. "Plan B. We're cutting it, and you're wearing a hat."

My entire body tenses and I start looking for plants or any semblance of nature to aid me.

"May I just wear the hat, Matt?" I ask. "We have not seen anyone following us for a while, and I do fancy my hair, you know?"

"No. Buzz it off," Matt replies with a deeper commanding voice in this new form.

Maybe he changes it at will to get others to be more pliable?

"While we cut it, tell me what the issue is with your wings or your magic."

"It is not really magic, Matt. It is feeling one with nature and flowing its energy to have it do what you will," I explain.

"But unfortunately, I do not feel that connection now, and I do not have a fae staff to ground myself."

Talking through my anxieties helps. "It is odd, but it is not, simultaneously. I know I visit the human realm frequently, and, of course, I do not bring a staff because my father only allows me get away with so much. He is not about to let such an important item be used recreationally."

"Speaking of which, didn't you say he'd be looking for you? If so, shouldn't we go back to where you woke up?" Matt asks while cutting my hair.

"I am not sure. The last thing I remember was arguing over something, over someone, then him pointing his staff at me. There was a flash of light, and the next thing I know I am in a park."

"Oh. I'm … I'm sorry, Elior. I know how shitty parents can be," Matt says from behind me while looking at me through the mirror.

I feel my mouth tighten and eyes narrow. "He is not immoral. He has always shown me kindness and love, and, in turn, I have shown him the respect he deserves as my father and a leader."

Matt's eyes widen, and he holds both hands up in recoil.

"Chill. It's not that serious," Matt says, taken aback. "Also, how is your dad going to repay me for my bike if he is trying to kill you?"

My jaw drops. "He is not trying to kill me. How dare you insinuate such things of him." A couple of guys look in our direction. "The fact that I do not remember what the argument was about does not erase years and years of being a doting father and king. If I know him like I do, he will be elated to see me return, will clarify all this for me, and will repay you in gold. We have no use for it other than creating durable items," I add in a lower voice.

Alex drops the shears and turns to me, face to face. "Hold up! You're fae royalty? You're a *prince*?"

"Yeah," I reply softly.

"What does that mean? Why are you here, then?"

It is conversational whiplash, and it takes me a moment to find an earnest answer to Matt's question.

"I know I came here often in recent times, which is odd for our kind. But if I did, it must have been at his direction I think."

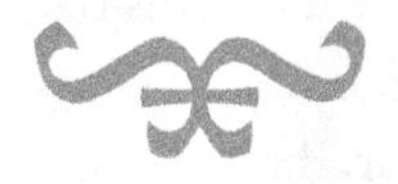

CHAPTER 5

Quarrel

Matt changes back to the Dana form as we exit the locker room. I've changed into some mud-colored shorts, a sky-blue long-sleeved shirt that I've rolled up to my elbows, and a black baseball hat. Dana cut just enough of my hair for it not to show prominently under the hat, which is a relief. My people talk about my pink hair, and I sort of like that my appearance is all the introduction I need in Lempara.

As we walk down the stairs, we spot two of the three goons who were chasing us earlier, now talking to the front desk girl.

"Oh, shit," Dana and I say in unison.

"Yes, that's him, right?" we hear the front desk girl say, pointing at me from below.

The two men in suits, now cleaned up and without sunglasses, have crew-cut haircuts. The one with green eyes and a large nose is built heavier than the other. The smaller one is oddly pale with olive-colored skin, snake-like dark features and eyes, and blond hair. They're both walking hastily toward Dana and me.

"You're on your own on this one," Dana chuckles nervously as she turns around and starts walking away.

"That's them all right," the smaller goon says. "Let's move."

The men rush up the stairs, and I flinch. If I run, they'll quickly catch up, and I'm not sure there's another way out of here. I must fight.

I have an advantage at the top of the stairs. That's when I notice the big goon slap on a metal attachment to his knuckles, and the smaller one whip out what seems like a metal fae staff.

Advantage over; they have weapons. There's no fighting. It's now a game of can't let them touch me.

I grab the locker-room floor sign to use as a weapon, but it's heavier than expected. So, I just aim for the big goon's head and swing as hard as I can. He dodges, but the sign hits him on the shoulder. His eyes narrow in anger. The smaller goon's mouth is agape, incredulous at what I just did.

"What the hell is going on?" I hear the front desk girl scream as she runs out the door we came in through.

The goons are within arm's length, so I just go for it. I jump down the stairs, throwing a kick to the big goon's chest. Ready for it, he dodges, but my effort isn't wasted. His smaller partner behind him takes the brunt of my kick. We fall down the stairs as I intended. Maybe I can make a run for the door.

As I stumble off the smaller goon, I hear him scream orders to the bigger one. "Get the other one, I'll deal with him."

Alex! I can't leave her.

The smaller goon is now on his feet and holding a baton

in his right hand. He turns to me. "You have no idea what's coming to you, pretty boy."

He lunges toward me, swinging the baton from the back, aiming for my head. I duck and grab his right arm with my right hand. He swiftly punches my stomach with his left hand. I flinch and release his right arm, giving him another opening for a strike.

"You're not even trying," he says. "I was told you could perform magic."

He strikes my face with the electric baton. It is the most intense pain I have ever felt. The burning sensation seems to take away all my energy. I fall to the floor.

"Who are you?" I ask between heavy pants for air.

He kicks me and smiles. "Your friend, Eva, sent us."

Eva. Her ivory skin, long brunette hair, big doe-like blue eyes, and sweet smile grinning back at me. Why is this name conjuring an image of a stranger in my mind?

"Eva?" I whisper to myself. He kicks me again in the chest. I can't help feeling betrayed, but I'm unable to pinpoint the culprit.

As the goon stands over me with a raised hand, ready to blow another strike with his electric rod, I muster enough strength to kick directly up and hit his left knee.

He drops the rod and falls backward. A rush of adrenaline surges through me. My instinct is to grab the weapon, but it seems to still buzz with man-made lightning. I grab a chair and hold it over my head to throw at him.

At this point, people are scurrying out of the lobby or running out of the gym altogether.

"Who is Eva? And why are you trying to kill us?" I demand, lowering the chair.

"You disgusting freak," the goon screams back. "We're not trying to kill you—not you at least. The morphing girl is just a bonus."

A shiver passes through my spine as I remember Alex.

Anger, anxiety, and an urge to throw up wash over me like a waterfall. I slam the goon with the chair and leave him writhing in pain. I can't bring myself to hit him in the head, I'm afraid it would cause irreversible damage.

"She is not a *girl*, idiot."

It's time to find Dana—or Alex. As I tremble while mounting the stairs, some of the gym-goers rush down seeking an exit.

"You don't want to go up there, dude," a muscular older man pleads with me. "I think a man just killed someone. We need to call the police."

Oh no! Please don't let it be Alex.

I climb the stairs faster and push the pain in my face to the back of my mind. As I near the top, a woman grabs me by the shoulders.

Dana—Alex!

"We have to leave," she says, half commanding, half trembling.

I grab her hands. "Indeed, but I could not leave without you."

"Aw. That's gross. And sweet, I guess. But I'm pretty sure I just killed a man, so we *really* need to get out of here right now."

"You what?" I yell.

The world becomes small and focused for a moment. It is just Dana and me. The danger of being captured is dwarfed by the notion she may have taken a life while I was trying to help her.

"Where's the other one?" Dana asks with a nervous smile, which takes me out of my own mind.

"I think I broke his knee, so stairs might not be his thing," I say quickly, trying to get back to the major transgression. "I cannot believe you killed—"

I interrupt mid-sentence so that I can duck a weight plate coming straight for our heads.

"Oh. Guess I didn't kill him after all," Dana jokes. "Hey, Frankenstein, you missed!"

Alex, now back as Matt, picks up the weight, and hurls it at the bigger goon.

"No!" I yell involuntarily.

"What? What do you mean *no*?" Matt inquires as he turns to me with a scrunched-up frown. "He's trying to kill us, Elior."

"Well … *you* perhaps. Not me. But that is not the point," I explain. "We cannot just have such a casual disregard for life."

"What are you talking about? This is self-defense," Matt says as he lands another blow at the goon with a smaller weight.

"We can just leave. Not every situation demands a reaction. You always have a choice," I say as I pull him by the arm backward toward the stairs.

"Not when they're trying to hurt you, Elior. Things are not always that simple," Matt says sternly. His eyes are shining. "You think I like this? This guy was going to kill me."

"He is down now! We can just leave."

"And what? Run? He found a changeling. I don't know if you've noticed, but I'm really good at leaving a situation. But sometimes, you must fight back. Things have a way of catching up to you."

"Maybe, but that is just not me. I think we should go now."

"Fine. Let's go," Matt pushes me ahead with force.

Matt changes his form back to the one from when I first met her. Her blonde female-presenting form. "This from the guy who broke someone's knees downstairs," she whispers loud enough for me to hear.

We spot the emergency exit on the second floor and make a run for it, rushing past the knocked-out goon on the floor. We pass by twenty benches and machines, with scared people hiding behind them. My heart sinks even further. This isn't me. I'm not the guy placing everyone's lives in danger and making them feel scared. I'm the one who makes things right and places people at ease—in any realm.

As Alex pushes the door open, we hear a loud banging sound. She screams in pain and flinches. I look back and see the woman from the murdering trio with a gun in hand and another, shorter woman next to her.

Eva.

CHAPTER 6

Clicking

"Alex! I am so sorry," I keep repeating, "I am so, so sorry."

"It's OK, Tinker Bell," Alex grunts as her leg keeps changing colors. "It was just a rubber bullet, and I heal fast. I'll be all right."

Alex was shot in the back of her leg. The bullet, thankfully, bounced off, and I am able to throw Alex's hand over my shoulder, jam the door, and escape the building with her.

We manage to walk through alleyways for about four blocks until we stop at one with the least amount of foot traffic. We are in a trash alley behind what I surmise are banquet halls or rest-something as humans call them. I still haven't eaten, and the smells around me remind my stomach of that fact.

Alex's morphing became unstable as soon as the bullet hit her, and her hair keeps changing color and her skin tones flip through all possible hues.

"You keep changing colors," I say to fill the silence.

"Did you know I'm one of the few people who can

answer whether a kick to the nuts or childbirth is more painful?"

"Is that true?"

"Not really, but it made you focus on something else, didn't it?" Alex says, smiling through the pain. "There we go. All good. Now, who the hell shot me, Elior?"

My heart skips a beat, and I feel the ground under my feet tremble in tandem. Wait—the ground—I feel it. Even if just for a fleeting moment, I feel a connection again to nature.

"Hello? I just asked you a question. Also, you have a weird grin on your face. It's making me so uncomfortable right now."

"I—I am sorry, Alex. I do not know the name of the woman who shot you. She was the same one chasing us this morning. But I think I know the girl with her. The bad guy with the lightning stick said her name, and it just clicked. It is Eva."

Bending at the knee to sit on the floor, I see the ground tremble a bit then pop up to make a small seat for me. Lowering myself to the ground, I smell the filth and decay around us. However, I ignore the olfactory discomfort to enjoy a moment of connection to this tattered earth.

"Oh my god! So many questions right now," Alex exclaims as she settles as a red-oak skinned female with delicate features, shoulder-length wavy black hair, and a strong runner's build. She is wearing slim jeans and a green hoodie, which seems to mimic the style of the people we passed along the way. "Who is—"

"Wait," I interrupt. Still sitting on my stump. "What do I call you in this form?"

Alex cocks her head and hip to the left and crosses her arms. "I don't know, I just took from the people we passed. Just go with … Leslie. I'm not too fond of that name or this form."

After thinking about her form for a second, Leslie snaps back. "Which bad guy and what lightning stick led to this epiphany of minuscule proportions?"

"Leslie, come on, what other bad guy could it be? The smaller one I graciously saved you from. He happened to have a lightning stick. It did not exactly *shoot* lightning, per se, but it felt like it when it hit me."

"I am *literally* flooded with questions every time you open your mouth, you pink-haired Muppet," Leslie says mid sigh. "How do you even know what lightning feels like?"

"Well, I have never been struck by lightning myself, but that is how you punish rule-breaking faes. Physical harm does not do that much damage to us. So, officials usually conjure up a storm in the hopes for lightning to administer punishment."

"So, you're weak against electricity. Got it. Good thing this is all happening 300 years in the past," snarks Leslie. "Why is there a stump of your making on the ground? Is that your magic?"

The stump does look out of place in the grim alley. A pop of brown dirt dug up from beneath a layer of suspect liquids and rat droppings.

"Again, not magic—but yes that was me. I am not sure how it happened, but I feel a small connection with nature again. I think my connection to nature is shaky because I do not have full access to my memory. As soon as the lightning-stick bad guy mentioned Eva's name, I felt something. Then when I saw her, the feeling became stronger," I stand up, coming face to face with Leslie. "Maybe I should just talk to her and see if she can clarify some of the memory lapses I have."

"Yes, yes, always an option," Leslie says while stroking her chin and putting a hand on her hip. "Only she was with the people trying to kill us, you idiot!"

"About that … lightning stick said she actually *hired* them," I sink back into my stump. "I do not think she wants to kill us. Well, me, at least. Lightning stick said they were looking for me, and you were just a bonus."

"My, my, my," Leslie huffs with one hand over her heart. "Those goons really know how to make me feel like the belle of the ball. But for real, who is this Eva? And can you remember why she's looking for you?"

"I do not remember who she is exactly, but I know I trust her, or did, I guess—given the circumstances. Maybe this is a misunderstanding, and she is just trying to help me."

"Is she human?" Leslie asks pointedly.

My eyes roll up, trying to remember her appearance. "She is not fae."

"How would a human know you?"

"Um. Great question, Al—Leslie," I stand and start pacing around. "As I mentioned, recently I have visited the human realm often, and while I try not to interact too much with humans, it is sometimes inevitable."

"Why are you getting all weird about that, Katy Perry?"

"Who is that?"

"Doesn't matter. Don't start deflecting, Fairy Prince!" Leslie quips.

"It is fae, not fairy. I have said that already," I bemoan, trying to buy time. Leslie just sneers at me. "Fae are not supposed to cross, according to the covenant."

"Oh, dear lord, this is going to take all day. You're a ridiculous person—says the changeling to the fae prince. Is Eva the police or something, then?"

"I do not think so. Because of the covenant, my father banned faes from crossing to the human realm many moons ago—I am not sure—like 400 or 500 human years ago. So, the humans who signed the covenant are likely gone because they do not live that long. And, even then, a fae had not crossed into this realm in a long time, so there was no need for human guardians."

"So, you're breaking your own laws? Finally, some interesting aspect to you other than the wings stuck to your back."

"Sort of. I did ask my father for surveillance permission to cross some time ago. He is the only one who holds a staff strong enough to open a portal. I had not seen the human realm since I was a child before the covenant was signed. I persuaded him by saying I would come in an official capacity, which would explain the lack of fae artifacts and my wings being retracted. I do know for certain that when I arrived, I fell in love with it. It is not my first time here."

"You fell in love with New York?" Leslie asks incredulously and then lets out a screeching cackle. "You are such a cliché, my prince. But why are you all freaked out?"

Leslie keeps laughing and sits down on my stump, while I move to the same place she was standing.

"The fae realm has aptly kept its connection to the earth, but the human realm has also done wonders. I found it vastly interesting and wondrous when I came back on my surveillance mission, so I think I kept returning without my father's knowledge."

"OK, so you think your father—the king of fae—will repay me in gold for returning a rule-breaking hell-raiser? You are unbelievable. I'm not going to get my money, and I'm over here being hunted for fun!"

Leslie remains in place on the stump, arms crossed, and her skin blood red.

"Yes, of course, he will," I reply, crouching down next to her, ignoring the lingering cats around us. "At the end of the day, I am the prince, and it is in his—and the kingdom's—interest that I return safely. Regardless of how he might feel about me after he learns of my indiscretions."

My knees sink to the floor. The connection to nature is now a bit stronger, so I will some vines and flowers to grow around the stump Leslie is sitting on to create a small throne for her.

"Just, please, point me in the direction of the portal? This is my only infraction of the covenant laws. I am a good monarch to my realm and always follow my king's rules. He will be understanding." At this point, it's more of a plea than a polite request.

Since I woke up that morning, it had been one confusing situation after another. Leslie—Alex—is the only familiar thing willing to help. And, I feel responsible for the multiple murder attempts against her. The least I can do is repay her for her effort and forced kindness. Although, I'm not sure if we still have gold in Lempara.

"Fine. Where's the portal?" Leslie says, laying back in her flower throne in her now red-oak skin again.

A broad smile materializes. "New York City!"

"Where in New York, Lewis and Clark?" Leslie says absentmindedly.

She keeps calling me different names, and I'm not sure what it means.

"I do not know. If I had my dad's staff, I think I could find it easily. Do humans still have seers?"

"See-what?"

"Seers—humans who can connect with spirits and nature. They used to be able to provide communication with loved ones in other realms and see a person's life path. Do you still have those?"

Leslie closes her eyes, and a smile tugs at her face.

"Come with me. I have an idea."

"Can we stop to get some food on the way?"

CHAPTER 7

Seer

"Here we are," Leslie says in sad triumph, pointing to an establishment below ground level with an illuminated bright sign of hands over an orb.

We have been walking for blocks, and all Leslie has said is that we were going to a seer or, as they are called, a "tarot reader."

The neighborhood we are in seems cleaner. More people are on the streets, which simultaneously gives me anxiety over being followed without us noticing, and some comfort of being able to blend in with the crowd.

We arrive at a building that is older and decrepit but juxtaposed to the breezy afternoon, it doesn't seem so scary, especially with constant foot traffic around.

"Is this where we can find a seer?" I ask eagerly.

"No, it's where we're going to clip your wings off, you overgrown dragonfly," Leslie says in a mocking tone.

"I sense sarcasm. I know what sarcasm is, Leslie."

"Do you also sense the tears of joy I'm crying that I don't have to explain basic human interactions to you?"

"No. But I sense hunger again."

In Leslie's defense, we did stop by some fruit trees on the walk over, and she bought some food boxes from some young children in matching green outfits.

"Oh my god, we can get more food after you talk to the witch and find out where the portal is," Leslie groans while walking in a circle.

My heart starts racing immediately.

"Wait … Leslie, is this a witch or a seer?"

"What's the difference?" she says, narrowing her frown.

"There is a big difference between a seer and a practitioner of dark magic."

"What? You're a practitioner of magic."

"I told you it is not magic. What faes do is energy shifting. Witches and warlocks are humans who try to mimic what we do by drawing on dark energy."

Leslie remains stoic for a few seconds, then bursts out laughing. My face remains so tense that not even lightning could crack it.

"I'm not even sure if this is a seer or a witch. It says there," as she points at the bright sign, "that her name is Ms. Jessica, and she's a tarot reader. How am I supposed to know about your weird pet peeves? And right now, she's the closest thing we have to some help."

"It is fae custom not to trust dark magic wielders. They draw energy from emotion and life, and death. Being part of the royal court, I was taught to set the example and thus denounce all dark magic and its wielders."

"Well, you're not in your court or your realm for that matter. And I don't even know if this is going to work, but we might as well try," Leslie says, her exasperation growing. "I'll be honest here—I need the money. But if you're not willing to try an alternative to find your stupid portal, then I'm out."

Leslie's words sound like the crackling of a dying fire. The flame of enthusiasm is extinguishing, and the promise of an unspecified reward isn't enough for her to stick around.

I stand in shocked silence, trying to reconcile what I was taught with what the right thing is to do at the moment.

Leslie rolls her eyes and sighs. "Have it your way, your majesty. I'm out. Thanks for almost getting me killed."

As she starts walking away, my heart beats faster, and my throat clenches. I reach out, saying, "Please do not leave," and I'm able to stop Leslie's body from moving—without touching her.

"What in the hell, Elior?" she yells.

She's not pleased with what I did. But, to my credit, I wasn't sure I had regained enough of my power back for it to work.

"I am sorry, it is just a minor pull," I explain. "I just held back the water in your body, thus, your entire body," I explain as I grin sheepishly.

"It's incredibly invasive, and you should never *ever* take control over someone's body without their permission," Leslie yells. "That being said—that's a hella cool power, Tinker Bell, and could've come in handy when we were being attacked!"

"I know. I am sorry," I bow my head. "I will talk to Ms. Jessica."

CHAPTER 8

Reading

The room is garish and bright for being underground. Every surface seems to be covered in brightly colored throws and pillows. Ms. Jessica looks nice enough. But dark wielders often do, as fae are taught. She is sporting a dark-toned tie-dyed sundress and a flower crown over her wavy brown hair.

"Welcome," Ms. Jessica says, in the husky voice of an older woman. "Looking to know your future?"

"Why yes, we are," Leslie says with a sweet twang in her voice. In the span of walking down the steps and crossing the threshold to the tarot reader's establishment, Alex has changed to a petite blonde wearing a short sky-blue summer dress that resembles an upside-down tulip. "But I'm awfully scared of these matters, ma'am. Is this like … dark magic or somethin'?"

Ms. Jessica looks sternly at Alex but softens her gaze. This charming form Alex took is disarming. She cannot only change her physical appearance but also embodies a new persona. It's amazing to watch. Changelings, from what faes have been taught, can usually just change into a few forms.

Yet, Alex can change at whim to whatever form she chooses. Truly exceptional.

"My dear, there's no 'dark magic' here—no need to worry. I have great intuition and the God-given gift of sight. For only $29.99, I can read what the cards say your future holds," Ms. Jessica explains while sitting at her table. "Or we could read both your cards for $50," she says, looking in my direction. "What do you say, handsome?"

"Oh, thanks so much, ma'am. That's so kind of you," Alex says in a cheerful tone that's just infectious.

But humans trade in paper, and neither of us have much. I didn't have any, and after the trip to the store and food earlier, Alex groaned about the lack of dollars. I'll just have to follow her lead, uncomfortable as I felt.

"Wonderful. Who's up first?" Ms. Jessica pulls a deck of long cards.

Alex gives me a reassuring look before volunteering to go first. I think that's her way of putting me at ease and showing me there's nothing to worry about.

After shuffling the deck a few times, Ms. Jessica places it on the table and asks Alex to break it into three equal stacks. Then, she repeats the process, asking Alex to do it thrice. After that's done, Ms. Jessica pulls a single card, claiming it as the "significator" or the card meant to represent Alex: The Judgement.

Ms. Jessica turns up the first card and places it on top.

"This covers you, dear. This is what you are going through right now."

The upside-down Hanged Man.

"Selfishness," she explains. "You've learned a lot about

yourself recently, but you're stalling to make an important decision. You've surrendered yourself to the greater good, even though you don't know what that means yet. Am I right?"

Alex's eyes narrow but she forces a smile back to the seer.

"This is your obstacle. Oh, the three of cups. Seems like you're embarking on a journey to figure out what that greater good is."

She turns another card and places it above the significator.

"This crowns you," Ms. Jessica says. "King of cups. Fairness and divinity. These are ideals you want to possess but are not yours yet."

The bright smile on Alex's face becomes harder to maintain and is replaced with a curious look with every new card placed on the table.

Ms. Jessica pulls another card and places it below the rest. The upside-down king of swords. That must be good.

Ms. Jessica purses her lips, and Alex's eyes fixate on hers.

"What is it?"

"This is beneath you. That which you have to work with," she says. "Evil intentions and breach of faith."

As she says those words, Ms. Jessica glances at me, making Alex turn her head to face me as well. While Ms. Jessica's expression holds contempt, Alex's is reassuring.

The seer turns another card and places it to her right.

"The seven of swords. This is behind you. And it's good that it is—counsel and babbling. As I see, you are embarking on a journey, and you'll need to rely on your own instincts."

She pulls another and places it to her left.

"This is before you. The four of pentacles. You will come into some inherited possession. Maybe of your family?" she jokes.

Ms. Jessica then draws four cards, and, one by one, she places them in a vertical line to her right.

"This is your attitude—two of cups. You're looking for love or romance. This is your environment—page of swords. You're in examination mode, looking for somewhere to belong. These are your hopes and fears—the knight of pentacles. You fear not serving a purpose."

Ms. Jessica looks up at Alex, who has two glossy eyes and an invisible dam holding back emotion. Surely, Alex is afraid of being caught but enough to break character?

"My dear—"

"That's enough, I think," Alex says with a smile that breaks the dam and lets one rebel tear out of their eyes and down their cheek.

"Are you sure? We only have one card left," Ms. Jessica prods. "And it's an important one—what will come."

Alex gets up from the chair with a forced smile.

I look closer and see the upside-down ten of cups. That doesn't look so scary. I do not understand how a few cards can make someone emotional.

Faes were taught that seers would assess someone's future through touch. Why was this woman reading playing cards then? This was turning out worse than meeting a dark magic wielder. This was a sham.

"Ready, young man?" Ms. Jessica asks, looking in my direction. Alex's eyes read of disappointment, juxtaposed with a reassuring smile. We both know this is a dead end. My only thought is how to get out of here without paying. I'm thinking I should stall Ms. Jessica until Alex comes up with a plan.

"Why not?" I sigh, resigning myself to whatever fate Alex brings me.

Ms. Jessica stays seated at the table but extends her hand to hold mine. Having spent so much time talking directly to Alex, I must seem like an entirely new person than the one who walked in. I place both my hands on Ms. Jessica's, as is fae custom, instead of the handshake humans prefer. She instantly recoils as if my hands were covered in thorns.

"You …" Ms. Jessica says with wide eyes and a shocked tone. "You're not … you're not human."

Alex stands from their chair. My heart sinks.

"How … how do you know?" I ask while running through the different scenarios this could turn into.

Faes were not, under any circumstance, to reveal themselves to humans. It is another rule of the covenant. And it's why my father banned us from crossing realms. Could that be why I don't remember anything? Was I cast out? Nonsense. No fae could erase memories. I am the prince of fae—heir to my kingdom.

Ms. Jessica is on her feet now, holding her hands close to her chest and backing away from me. "I don't know. You just don't feel human. I'm not sure how to explain it."

"Ms. Jessica, we are not here to hurt you," I explain, taking slow steps toward her. "I just need some help finding my way."

"I—I bought that card deck online and started this shop

in my basement. I live upstairs. My grandmother was the one with the true gift of sight. I don't think I can help you 'find your way.' I'm sorry."

Ms. Jessica is visibly uncomfortable, shaking as she confirms my suspicions of her lack of ability. But she *was* able to sense I wasn't human.

"He literally meant find his way—as in a physical place to go," Alex interjects. "We're just trying to get him home, ma'am. Apparently, they travel through portals, and there's one in New York."

Ms. Jessica seems relieved at the thought of directions and not spiritual guidance. "I don't have the gift. I'm sorry. I can't help."

All that stress for nothing. This is just a waste of time. "I understand. I am sorry to have troubled you in your residence."

She seems conflicted at the sight of us getting ready to leave. "Maybe there's someone else who *can* help," Ms. Jessica adds, as Alex and I head toward the door. "There's this group of tarot readers and mystics that meets regularly. But to be honest, I'm not sure any of them actually has the gift my grandmother did."

"Terrific lead, ma'am. We are, indeed, looking for more dead ends," Alex snarks.

"You really dropped that whole out-of-town sweet girl thing quickly, didn't you?" Ms. Jessica says pointedly.

"And you dropped the whole shivering scared bit," Alex retaliates.

"What I was trying to get at is that when we meet, the conversation usually turns to this one young girl who many of them believe is the real deal. I think she's actually a seer or a witch of some sort. She works in the East Village."

She's not even sure what type of person she's recommending, and we're not even sure who we're taking a recommendation from. This is ludicrous. It's one thing to go see a potential dark magic wielder in hopes of it being a seer. It's another to have a fake seer send us to talk to a likely dark magic wielder. It is what I call a dead end.

"Great. Do you have a name and address?" Alex asks cheerfully.

"Sure. And I'm sorry I can't be of more help," Ms. Jessica says as she turns to a small table near me with a pen and paper. "What *are* you, though?"

Alex and I lock eyes and, without her having to utter a word, I know it is my turn to take command. I give her a nod, acknowledging that I can handle Ms. Jessica's inquiry smoothly without revealing too much—to avoid making any of us a target for those chasing us.

"I am Elior—prince of the fae realm of Lempara," I say, bowing my head. "And we thank you for your assistance, if incomplete and insufficient."

If Alex could change her eyes into spikes and shoot them at my head, I believe she would at that exact moment.

Alex forces a laugh. "What Eric means is that he's also a warlock and needs to travel to his realm."

"He's no warlock," Ms. Jessica says to Alex while handing over a note. "And I'm no seer, but his touch felt like grabbing a tree or burying your feet in the sand or feeling the rain fall on you. From what I'm told, warlocks and witches don't feel that way."

"Besides," she adds while handing Alex the note, "witches and warlocks have no other realm or purpose than to make this one a living hell."

Ms. Jessica is my favorite human right now.

"You hear that, Alex? Told you dark magic wielders are no good."

I turn to her with a big smile only to meet the now red-faced and frowning Alex.

My sense of superiority quickly turns to guilt. I know I have done something to upset Alex. All I want to do is immediately apologize, but I am afraid of making it worse.

"It's time to leave, *Elior*," she says sternly and loudly.

Ah—the name. She's mad because I used our names.

I bow in gratitude to Ms. Jessica as Alex walks past me to the door.

"She's right, you know," Ms. Jessica says to me, following Alex with her gaze. "Names are a powerful thing. From her reaction, I gather those are your real ones?"

"Yes," I sheepishly admit.

"A name calls your being. It draws your energy when spoken. Having someone know your name means you're giving that person access to your attention and focus," Ms. Jessica explains. "I don't mean to be rude, but you strike me as the type of person who's had their name spoken in adoration. She hasn't had the same luck in the world. The cards are silly. But sometimes they can help you look at the obvious, and that girl is masking a lot of pain."

I am skeptical about what Ms. Jessica is saying about Alex. Still, it makes me realize I know very little about the person helping me find my way home.

"She doesn't want the one thing she can protect taken away by people knowing who she is," Ms. Jessica added. "Or, at the very least, found. I'd be careful of her, if I were you, prince."

"'Careful of *her?*" I retort in a low protective tone. "You are wrong about her. She has shown me nothing but kindness—even if self-interested. Thank you again."

As I turn toward the exit, the butterflies in my stomach flutter so fast that I almost throw up. I must stand for my subjects, but I also hate confrontation—especially when Ms. Jessica's words resonate with me.

I look to the door as I'm walking out, and Alex jolts back in, pale-faced and out of breath.

"They found us. They're here," she says.

CHAPTER 9

Hiding

Alex is panting, with her back against the door. Her gaze is fixated forward.

"They're here," she repeats. "Four of them. Your friend Eva, too."

My chest feels almost too small for my heart. And I'm so frustrated that I just want to curse out loud and let the tears start falling. But there's no time for that.

"Did they see you?" I exclaim.

My question comes off more accusatory than I intend it to be.

Alex fixates her gaze on mine with the same frown she last left me. "Of course, they saw me, idiot. I'm not invisible. But they haven't seen this form, so I don't think they suspect anything. They were walking in this direction, though."

Ms. Jessica breaks the tension with a barrage of questions and a displeased tone. "Now, who in the hell is coming here? And why are you two so scared? I don't want any trouble in my store."

She was right; we unknowingly brought a group of

violent goons right to her doorstep. I debate whether to lie to her and try to sneak out—and probably get caught—or just level with her and hope that she will help us one more time.

I go with my instinct.

"Ms. Jessica, we do not know why they are chasing us, but they tried to harm us both twice now. I understand you do not owe us anything, and you have already helped us. But is there any way you would let us hide here until they are gone?" I say bluntly while kneeling on one leg and bowing my head. "Please, I appeal to your kindness."

"Boy, you do not have to be so dramatic," Ms. Jessica replies, rolling her eyes. "But I don't want any trouble in my store."

"I completely understand. If there is a way to hide us and wave them away, there is no need for an altercation."

Alex kneels right next to me, mimicking my pose. We're at Ms. Jessica's mercy now.

She seems unsure but ultimately agrees with a heavy grunt. "Just hide here in this closet and don't make a damn sound."

Ms. Jessica lifts one of the drapes to uncover a small screened door that clearly has not been painted or dusted in quite some time.

"And you, little Miss Country," Ms. Jessica says to a baffled Alex as she sits down at the table. "If you're so sure these men chasing you didn't recognize you, just come sit back down and let's continue your reading."

Bad idea, I think. Alex is an amazing changeling, but we still don't know who these people are and how good they'll be at spotting one. Plus, it places an insurmountable pressure on Alex who might break form from it.

"Maybe she can squeeze in here with—"

The door creaks open.

Alex promptly sits down, and I close the closet door. The drape falls and covers it, leaving me in complete darkness.

"Good afternoon, ma'am," says a deep masculine voice, which doesn't sound like the smaller goon who fought me at the gym. This must be the bigger one speaking. "Sorry to disturb you. We need to ask you and your client a few questions if you don't mind."

"It's very rude to interrupt a reading," I hear Ms. Jessica say. "Who do you think you are to gang up and barge into my business?"

"I'm Agent Matia Lange, with the FBI, and these are my associates," the deep voice says. "As I said, I need to ask you both a few questions, and we'll be on our way."

"I'm sorry, officers. Have I broken the law by being here? Ah shoot, I knew I shouldn't have come to this ungodly place." Alex goes into full character with this form. Were we not in impending danger, I would laugh at how ridiculous she sounds.

"Miss, we saw you come in a few minutes prior to us arriving here. When you got in, did you see anyone else?" Lange asks Alex.

"Why no, no one at all. Just Ms. Jessica here. You see, I've recently moved to the city, and my boyfriend from back home told me he wasn't coming to visit this month and then broke up with me," she bursts into tears and heavy sobs. "I was just looking for some guidance or reassurance that I would be OK."

This is quite the smoke and mirrors show Alex is giving them.

"Miss, just step outside, please. We need to talk to Ms. Jessica," another voice says. I recognize this one as the smaller goon who smacked my face with that lightning stick.

My blood starts boiling at the sound of his voice. I do not want Alex to have to deal with that man. But at least Alex is leaving, and I'm in hiding. As long as I stay quiet, everything will be over soon, and Alex and I can continue to the portal. Well, a seer—then the portal.

After I hear the door close, Lange speaks again to Ms. Jessica. "We know two people we're looking for were here," he says and pauses. "Or are still here. And we need to know everything from how they arrived, what they said, what they looked like, and where they went."

"You came to the right place. I'm in the business of answering questions," Ms. Jessica replies to my astonishment. "Let me answer one for free, first. You're not FBI."

There's a small pause in the dialogue. Almost on beat, a feminine and strong voice says, "Look at that, you actually might be the real deal. Or you're just not stupid. What do you want? We're in a hurry."

"That depends; why are you looking for them?"

"We don't have time for this," Lange groans. "Varya, can I just take her out?" There's a clicking sound.

I hear a scuffle, and furniture falls to the floor.

The beat of the conversation continues.

"Two of them. But you don't know what they look like,"

Ms. Jessica's voice is still commanding but starting to get frail and shaky.

"One of them is male with tan skin and pink hair," Varya replies matter-of-factly.

"He was here with a girl," Ms. Jessica says, as my heart sinks.

"What did she look like?"

"You just asked her to leave."

A pause. A hit. A thud.

"Varya, really?" the smaller goon says. "Lange called it before you."

My lungs contract, and I try my best not to hyperventilate and make a sound. All that focus manifests as sweat. Any doubt I have about whether they were sent by my father to rescue me is erased. Faes are taught to value and honor life. We do not take lives. It is not our place in the ecosystem to make that decision.

"Shoto, shut up," Varya responds. "Lange would've made a mess and attracted attention. I handle things eloquently and discreetly."

"Yeah, like the little stunt you pulled back at the gym? That was eloquent."

"You and Lange decided to go in without my approval—"

"They were already leaving," the smaller goon, Shoto, interjects. "You should thank me for doing your job."

"I'm not wasting time with you. You and Lange go out and look for the morphing girl. Ms. Eva and I will catch up after we figure out where the target went."

"How? You took out our lead!"

I almost throw up. I realize I have to get out there

immediately. Alex is being chased by two likely murderers, and the brains of the operation will probably figure out where I am soon enough.

"There's a security camera outside. How stupid do you think I am, Shoto? Go. Now."

The door creaks again, and I hear the sounds of the two men's footsteps go out. A camera—I know what that is. A human showed me one on one of my visits. It is the most magical thing humans have created. The ability to capture what our eyes see into a physical object is something no fae had ever done. With a racing mind, I realize what is about to happen and what I have to do. But I have to bide my time.

"Ms. Eva, would you be so kind as to look for an office or computer while I make this look like a slip and fall?" Varya asks with the same ease as one would for a drink of water.

After some shoveling noises that I only imagine are the moving of furniture and the body of Ms. Jessica, tears start falling down my face. This is all just too much. I placed Alex in danger, and my life might end today in the underground room of a nice fake seer who I thought was a witch. How did I get myself into this situation?

I see a streak of light. They lifted the throw next to the one I am hiding behind.

"Here it is," Eva's voice sounds kind and sweet as ever.

More tears slip down my face. Why can't I remember anything about this person, yet I yearn for her voice? Water is dripping down my nose, and I battle every instinct to sniffle. I sense both Eva and Varya next to me. So close to what they're looking for, but so focused on their plan that it squeezes out room for the unexpected. I can use that to my advantage.

"This is way too much work. Remind me to up my fee," Varya says to herself and Eva. "You sure we can't just follow them to where they're going if you just want to find the portal?"

"I have no use of a locked door if I don't have the key. He's the key … or at least, part of him is," Eva says in a soft voice with a twinge of annoyance.

They need me, but they're not looking for me. They're looking for Lempara.

I thought humans had forgotten about our realm; relegating it to fables and history. What possible business could humans want with the fae realm? Destroy it as they're doing to their own? I can't let people with this little regard for life get near the portal to Lempara.

"Let's see," Varya says to herself. "OK, so here they are coming in. Ugh, I can't believe we let that morphing girl just slip through."

"She's secondary to this mission. Elior is our focus," Eva tells her.

Hearing Eva utter my name feels comfortable. It's as if she is looking for a friend.

"Morphing girl went out," Varya narrates. "I'm guessing that's when we see her because she goes back in, and we arrive."

The small silence is broken by the tearing of the throw next to mine.

"He either used the backyard entrance, or he's still here,"

Varya adds. She's so annoyed that she almost grunts the words.

"He's still here," Eva says calmly. "He's not one to take risks."

This is it.

As the throw I am standing behind is pulled down, I open the screened door and will the little air I can from the room to push the throw over Varya and Eva. It doesn't knock them over, but they become entangled enough for me to escape.

"I am sorry!" I yell as I run past them to the door.

CHAPTER 10

Run

As I make my way up the steps from Ms. Jessica's shop, I see a group of people gathering by the sidewalk in front.

I recognize Alex who is now disguised as Matt from the gym. He's OK and alive. I regain my breath, as Matt spots me from a few feet away. I keep running, grabbing him by the arm and taking turns down alleys as fast as I can.

"What was that about?" I ask as I begin slow down our pace. "Are you all right?"

"I'm actually more efficient without you dragging me down, *Elior*. I can handle myself, and that's what I did. The crowd was there wondering how two grown men were knocked down in broad daylight."

He is still mad about his name being revealed. He doesn't know what happened to the person it was revealed to.

"Matt, I am so sorry," I say through tears that have not stopped pouring. "I think they killed Ms. Jessica, and now I know that what they really want is me. They need me to open the portal."

If this revelation surprises Matt, he gives no indication.

His frown and pursed lips remain intact. As macabre as I know it is, I was hoping forgiveness for my transgression would've been immediate after he learned of Ms. Jessica's murder.

"But you don't even know where it is," he relents. "Let alone how to open it."

"I do not think they care. And I think they are interested in you now, too."

I know that by telling him that piece of information, I run the risk of him leaving me to fend for myself. As he has said, I'm the one dragging him down. He has done so much already: he should leave now that he has the opportunity.

We stop a few blocks away from Ms. Jessica's store, and we hear a few sirens in the distance. By now, the body must have been found by the human guardians.

"We have to find a charger," Matt says while inspecting our surroundings.

That was not the response I was expecting. "A charger?"

"Yeah, for my phone. We need the maps tool to route our way to this seer if we want to find the portal before those thugs find you."

He's staying with me. The tears resume, and I throw myself at Matt to hug him.

PART II

CHAPTER 11

Answers

After releasing him from my grip, Matt changes back to his Leslie form with her skinny jeans and a green hoodie. We walk to a nearby coffee shop. It is small and provides a backroom sitting space we take advantage of to escape any possible street surveillance by the "Fearsome Four," as Leslie calls them.

As I tell her what happened after she left Ms. Jessica's store, I explain how I seem to remember Eva's voice and was able to move wind again, if ever so lightly.

"I knew you were magic, dude," Leslie says with a smugness that would be irritating from anyone else. "Can you do something now?"

"I am not sure. I can feel a faint connection to the earth. But other than creating simple stumps or gusts of wind, I am not sure I am able to bend nature too much. It is frustrating."

It is one of the hardest things I've had to face. Without my connection to the earth, I'm useless as a fae. And without a way back home, I'm hopeless as a monarch. I'm relying on a stranger's kindness to help me. What if I hadn't run into a changeling? The Fearsome Four would've hurt or captured me already. I feel completely useless.

Noting the expression on my face, Leslie scoots over the bench we are sitting on and places her arm on my back. She can't understand what I'm going through, but just being there is helping.

Being there! It dawns on me that I have no idea how Leslie, or Matt, or Alex, was able to fend off Lange and Shoto.

"How *did* you knock those goons out, Leslie?"

Leslie lets out a disruptive cackle and, for a small moment, looks embarrassed after other patrons turn their heads in our direction. She never looks embarrassed.

In a quieter voice, Leslie says, "It was the oldest trick in the book. And honestly, I'm disappointed in them, after they brought it so hard at the gym.

"I was skulking around the area after I stepped out of Ms. Jessica's, and I saw them come out. Now, I'll admit, they did catch me by surprise and spotted me, which is a rare thing for me. But that was my fault for staying in the same form. I wasn't sure this would work, but I tried to blend into my surroundings to camouflage and make a run for it and then something new happened. I think I turned invisible."

My eyes feel like they're about to pop out of my face and my mouth is far as open as can be. Changelings can change forms and only into a few of them at that. But Alex is able to change and modify in the blink of an eye and now play light games with her body. She's unpredictable and fearsome.

"How?" is all I'm able to manage.

A group of young humans with backpacks and books sits at the table next to ours. The group is in a deep loud conversation over someone being "blocked on social," whatever that means.

Leslie inspects every person in the group and proceeds in almost a whisper. "Yeah, I know. It's crazy! After I did that, the three of us were clearly confused. So, I pulled a Tom and Jerry and grabbed the smaller one's hand with the electric baton toward the big guy's face. After he fell and the small one began flailing his arms around, I just threw a rock at him. I took the electric baton once they were on the ground and zapped them for good measure."

"You should not take pleasure in causing pain, Leslie," I struggle to say. After all, she did that in self-defense.

She rolls her eyes in response and turns to the group of students. "Excuse me," Leslie interrupts them in a sweet voice, with her phone in hand. "Would any of you happen to have a phone charger I could borrow briefly? Mine just died."

"I think I have one," says a young boy as he hands Leslie a black block with a string. "We'll be here for a few hours, just let me know when your phone is powered up."

While Leslie connects her phone to the string and the block to the wall, she turns her attention back to our conversation. "What is it with you about violence, really? I can understand not wanting to hurt living beings out of nowhere, but what I don't understand is not wanting to hurt someone who's out to hurt you."

"It is more complicated than that, or maybe even simpler," I explain, not able to look Leslie in the eye and just focusing on a smudge on the table at which we are sitting. "I told you, it is not a fae's place to make decisions that impact a life. And I, especially, need to set that example as a monarch. Our entire existence and our realm are thanks to the tenets of life, spirit, and balance."

Leslie simply stares at me.

"Oh, I'm not interrupting. I'm finally getting some answers."

"Long ago, faes and humans shared a realm," I explain, still unable to look up at Leslie. "As humans started expanding their kingdoms, they began building more and more weapons to aid them in their missions. And, they willingly turned them against anything that threatened their own clans. They flattened forests, stopped rivers flowing, and excessively killed and enslaved fauna and even their own.

"Faes and humans usually had an amicable relationship. But after seeing the destructive path humans had embarked upon, a group of faes sought to take a stand in defense of those who were defenseless. After much pain and loss, the fae saw how humans took pleasure in fighting. They celebrated their opponents' deaths as if it did not implicate their own lives and the entire balance of the ecosystem. They lauded themselves after pillaging the land they walked on and proclaimed themselves kings and queens as if they were not abusing themselves in the process. So, the fae put together a peace treaty that divided the lands and regions for humans to pillage and for the fae to protect against them. The human leaders agreed to the covenant meeting, and, after long ineffective negotiations, the fae presented their last option. To create our own realm, close to the human's but not in the same space. This took the humans by surprise, but, ultimately, they agreed. That was covenant law. As I am told, the humans requested another meeting with the fae to review the details, and all parties agreed to come in a diplomatic capacity. Relieved that they were finally making some headway, the fae came to the meeting unarmed. Every single fae at the covenant gathering was without a weapon. In their defense, the humans left their own weapons as well. In their avarice, humans wanted the fae to create our realm but wanted free access between them for those in both groups to choose their preferred realm. The—"

Loud laughing from the students next to us takes me out of my story, and I look up at their table. As I reposition myself, I lock eyes with Leslie. They're fixated on me, intrigued, afraid to make a sound as to not interrupt me. It's disarming and endearing.

"The fae denied such demand, fearing the humans would try to just conquer a new realm," I continue, now just looking directly at Alex. "So, the humans ushered in their latest secret weapon—dark magic wielders—witches and warlocks as they later became known. It seemed that humans had already been working on their own version of redirecting energy as the fae do. Yet unable to do so with the energy of nature, they turned to the energy of death and human emotion. It was an ambush. All the fae present that day were slaughtered. As soon as the news of the massacre spread, coordinated attacks on fae from dark magic wielders began. My grandfather rallied all the fae he could reach and began the process of establishing our realm under a full moon. For two generations, the fae have been forbidden from coming back to this realm. But, as I told my father when I pleaded for a visit, our realms are related, and I wanted to see the conditions in which this one was."

"So, that's why you were apprehensive about meeting with a witch versus a seer," Leslie says, while she fiddles with her phone.

"Yes. They almost decimated my entire race of people," I say solemnly. "What is your story, though? Where did the motorcycle come from? And why are you here?"

"Maybe another time. Now we just have to pray this lady is a seer and not a witch. Otherwise, this meeting is going to be very awkward for you."

Leslie disconnects the string from her phone and the box from the wall. My nerves once again send their greetings to my chest and stomach.

"Can we get food on the way?" I ask Leslie sheepishly as she walks back from returning the string black box to the young boy at the next table.

She looks at me with wide eyes and a downward smile. "How opposed are you to some redistribution of wealth?"

CHAPTER 12

Sleepover

For the train ride to Manhattan, Alex changes to Matt's form, claiming it will be easier to navigate the city presenting as a male. He also reminds me what Manhattan is and how it is different than New York as a whole. It's all a very fascinating juxtaposition, compared with the fact that there is only one land in the fae realm.

Lempara exists with no borders within itself. All living beings are expected to live in harmony, and for those who don't, there are the lightning towers. Nothing more egregious than petty theft has ever occurred during my time there, and in most cases, it does not amount to a lightning punishment. But every few years, I hear the scuffle as they take someone—or something—up there. I try not to concern myself too much with those matters. After my father is gone, I'll handle those issues. Until then, I get to talk to the people and establish relations with the merchants across the land.

For a locked land with limited access, we do receive a number of beings from the human realm seeking refuge.

When a kraken comes in, or a merfolk tribe seeks asylum, the balancing process begins anew. That's where my mother and sisters come in—creating spaces and ecosystems that work in balance with the rest of the land.

I love when new beings are in the land. Watching the patterns and quirks that they developed in the human realm is fascinating. Each one of them enriches our land and are my inspiration to check out the human realm myself. Yes, most of them speak of atrocities that led them to Lempara. Still, amid all the human-caused pain, there's always something they miss about this realm that can't be recreated in the fae one. For some, it's the ingenuity brought on by humans. For others, it was the thrill of not knowing what would happen next.

As I explain to Matt in the underground wagon transporting us, I wanted to experience firsthand what uncertainty felt like. I got more than I bargained for, however.

"You don't remember anything before waking up in the park?" Matt asks, eyeing every person that jumps in or out of the wagon at every stop it makes.

"Yes and no. I have long-term memory, as you have noticed, I just cannot seem to remember how I got here. I remember asking my father's permission to come, and that is it," I say as I close my eyes, hoping to block out visual distractions and to recreate memories in my mind but nothing comes. "It feels, however, like I have been here recently. I recognized Eva's voice, and she knows me. And we do not have motorcycles or cameras in Lempara."

"The fact that the last thing you remember is your dad pointing his weapon at you makes me believe that he erased your memory because he was mad at you," he says plainly without looking at me.

"Nonsense. My father would never harm me. I have proven myself time and again as a son and a monarch. Besides, faes do not have the power to erase memories."

"I don't know, dude. All I'm saying is that sometimes the simplest answer is the correct answer."

"I guess we will find out when we visit the seer. Have you given any thought to what you would want to ask them?" I ask, trying to shift the conversation away from me and my family.

"Nope. Nothing at all," Matt replies so quickly it seems as if he was expecting the question. "I do have a question for you, though."

He turns to me. Eyes fixated on mine, almost containing a plea.

"Are there more like me in Lempara?" The words almost crawl back into his mouth as he says them. It is a real question. And it's coming from Alex. A moment of honesty—something I haven't seen from her all day.

I hesitate to answer the question. Not because I am afraid of the truth but because I want to phrase it in a way that will not hurt his feelings. It's mind-blowing how I met Alex this morning, and by the afternoon we have lived a whole life together. In the span of twelve hours, Alex has gone from wanting to kill me to protecting me, joking with me, feeding me, and caring for me. I owe her the same level of care for what I know is going to be disappointing news.

The wagon stops again. "Is this where we get off?" I ask

instinctively to fill the silence between us and buy myself some time.

Matt takes it as me not wanting to answer the question, and I see his embarrassment.

It's a bad habit of mine to try to divert situations until I'm ready to handle them. Whether it's changing the subject or redirecting energy around me, I always find a way to have interactions turn in a way that makes me comfortable, disregarding how blatantly transparent it is to other people or how that might make them feel.

"No. A few more stops," Matt says softly, turning his gaze back on the incoming passengers.

"There are none," I say, looking down. "To answer your question. There are no known changelings left. That is why I was so surprised when I met you. About two or three human decades—I am not sure, since time in the fae realm moves differently—the fae received word that changelings had become extinct. I am sorry, Alex. You may be the last of your kind."

Without skipping a beat, Matt turns to me with a big smile and teary eyes. "Figures. I guess I'm more special than I thought!"

Just as he can see through my evasiveness, I see through his smile.

Alex can simultaneously feel genuine and performative. Like a jester who enjoys his job at the beginning but has grown weary of the performance.

"I take it your parents are not changelings. I know it is not something necessarily passed down genetically, but have you asked them about any relatives who might be like you?"

My question is as welcome as a splash of cold water to the face.

"My, my, Nancy Drew, aren't we a little curious?" Matt says in jest but clearly turning tables because he's the one evading questions now. "But very astute. My parents are *not* like me. They made sure I remembered that."

The solemn tone of that last bit is my signal to not pry any further.

"This is us," Matt says in a low serious voice.

We exit the underground wagon and battle through a multitude of people—so many that it should be a public health hazard to have that many beings cramped together in underground tunnels.

We finally make it up the stairs to the ground level to find a dark night with flashing lights. The place seems familiar yet foreign. Like it was designed with high hopes but inevitably fell victim to humans.

It is some of the dirtiest air that I have ever breathed, and still you can feel so much vibrant energy around you. It isn't coming from the earth. It is coming from the sheer number of humans around you looking for someone, walking together, or cackling by a corner.

Matt is taking in the convoluted views as much as I am.

"Well, this is a good news/bad news situation," he says with a handsome smile, trying to be endearing.

And it's working.

"My phone says the place is a residence, so we have to wait until tomorrow to go there, and we still have the Fearsome Four after us," Matt says, exaggerating a pout.

"I am really hoping that is the bad news, you overgrown porcupine," I respond, trying to engage on his level.

"Oh! He's here!" Matt yells through a heartfelt cackle. "He has arrived, and he's got jokes, ladies and gentlemen!"

I am mortified, embarrassed, and sort of scared of the attention that Matt is bringing to us.

"But yes, that *is* the bad news," he concludes. "The good news is that we don't have money to rent a hotel room, so you're going to have to flex your fairy muscles to provide us some shelter for the night."

"I am sorry, what?"

"There's a park near where we're going and, given that I only have enough money for a few meals, I thought you could do a little cave in the dark of night or throw some vines over us. I don't know you. I don't know what you can do," he says in a jovial tone, grabbing both my arms. "Listen, you love eating, so this is in your best interest. I'm looking at you as a risky investment."

"I can try, but it is hard to shift energy with memory lapses and without a staff or working wings."

"That's the spirit! Unconvincing and noncommittal!" Matt smiles at me. "Like a true American."

"I have to say, Matt, I do not get most of your jokes. But I do realize you are trying to be funny."

Matt's face drops, and he stares me down for a few seconds. "That is *the* funniest thing you've said to me all day."

He beams and hugs me. "Let's go. God knows how long it'll take to find a secluded place, and for you to be of use."

CHAPTER 13

Flex

We wait for what seems like forever for the majority of people in this small park to clear. Over by the benches, a small group with tattered clothes starts gathering, but they are mostly focusing on the treasures of one's shopping cart.

Matt and I take our opening and walk into the tiny wooded area—if you can call it that, it is mostly overgrown bushes, but Matt keeps calling it the "woods of the park."

I am not about to complain. He did get food for us.

Now covered by the woods, Matt engorges his arms and hands and uses them to rake the forest floor.

"Well, that's the extent of my contribution to this endeavor, your majesty. Take it away," he gestures with both hands extended to me, accompanied by a charming smile.

"Take what away?"

"You know, do your nature-y thing. Build a bed of soft leaves or create a small tent with branches and stuff."

I can't help but think that this is mostly a test by Matt to see more of what I can do. Because I told him about the air manipulation, he brings up my energy shifts at any opening.

He even seems giddy about spending the night outside, which does not strike me as his preference.

He has turned this into a performance, and now I'm nervous.

"Be warned that my connection to nature and my spirit have been weak today," I add a disclaimer. "So please, do not take this as a reflection on me or my kind's balance with nature. We take our connection very seriously."

"Just get on with it!"

I take my shoes off and close my eyes. As I focus on my breathing, I pay attention to which direction the wind is blowing, how loose and moist the ground feels, what the temperature is, and the condition of the flora around me. To ask something of nature before acknowledging its state is foolish and dangerous.

This would be so much easier if I had a staff with me. I haven't done a big energy shift in a while, and at least then I could remember what I did the day before.

I stomp and ground my left foot forward and raise my arms to my chest simultaneously. The ground follows suit and lifts up a knee-high, bench-like formation. I meant for it to be more detailed, but the good news is I have some sort of connection back.

"Whoa! I didn't think you'd actually do it," Matt screams at first and then lowers his voice to not attract attention.

I repeat the same move for a second bench, and Matt continues to mouth something at me. His eyes almost jump out of his face in disbelief, as if his sense of sight is envious of touch for confirmation of reality.

It's cute. It's really bad form on my part, but Matt sees it as the greatest achievement. For a moment, I think of all the tricks I can show him once I get my hands on a staff and then quickly realize for that to happen would mean I'm no longer in this realm and Alex has received her payment.

I think my demeanor changes because Matt looks at me concerned, so I just quickly focus on the flora and will them to grow, expand, and shape themselves into a hut around the two ground benches to fully cover them.

"Sorry if I distracted you, Elior," Matt says in a husky low tone.

"Not at all! Just difficult without my wings expanded or a staff in my hands is all," I brush him off, successfully masking disappointment.

It's nonsense. I have only known this person for a day.

We walk into the small hut, and Matt lays down the small bag he was given at the food stand. As we try to settle ourselves to rest on our respective ground benches, he turns and asks about my wings.

"I do not understand," I admit. "I can usually retract and expand them at will, but I have not been able to move them all day. I rely on them a lot, not just for flying, but they also have their own connection to nature through the wind and rain. They serve as a guide sometimes."

As I say the words, it dawns on both of us.

"Your wings are a compass? Can they find the portal?" he asks.

"I think? I do not remember."

It's frustrating. And the worst part is not having anything or anyone to channel this frustration toward but myself. How can I remember so much of myself and my people, yet have no specifics on how I can go back home?

"Guess we figured out what I want to ask the seer," Matt says triumphantly.

"How to get my wings to work?"

"Nah. How to get those legs and not have to walk all the time," he says, staring at the lower half of my body before turning away from me to rest.

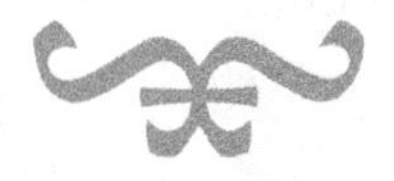

CHAPTER 14

Witchcraft

When we wake up, Alex decides to change to a new form. She settles on a female-presenting brunette with feathery hair going by the name of Farrah. She is to walk a few steps in front of me to not draw attention.

Alex's plan is not well-thought-out because Farrah, although short in stature, has a very beautiful face and actually draws second looks from every passerby. As we come up from the underground wagons, our walk is mostly silent. Occasionally, Farrah looks back to make sure I am keeping up and to flash me a cute smile—which she probably is flashing to everyone else because all who came across her smiles back.

The sun is glaring straight down on us, but the warmth feels like a comforting hug from a friend, encouraging me to go further. It'll all be over soon. I'll be back home before I know it.

"It should be one of these," Farrah says, looking from her phone to the buildings' numbers.

My heart starts beating fast again. The last time we

visited a seer, it ended in murder. I can't be responsible for another person's death, even if it turns out this is a dark magic wielder.

Farrah walks up to the door and knocks. No one answers.

I'm leaning against a tree that, like all the greenery in this city, has not been able to grow healthy.

The street is pretty deserted, except for a young woman walking a dog in our direction.

"Let's take a walk and come back again in an hour or so," Farrah says, turning in my direction and looking around.

"Elior," she says. "You're crying."

"Oh. Sorry."

It isn't until Farrah points it out that I feel the tears coming down my face.

Farrah comes closer and lowers her voice. "What's going on, Thumbelina?"

I know she is just saying it to liven the mood, but this time it rubs me the wrong way. Not just because I don't know the reference, but because I have so much pent up animosity that I am looking for any excuse to unleash it on someone.

"Nothing," I snap. "Your name-calling is getting a little tiresome, you know?"

I bite my tongue because I know that if I continue, I will say something I don't mean.

She just smiles. "Fair enough. I'll settle for Tinker Bell, but I'm not going to refer to you as Elior when we're actively being chased by the Fearsome Four. Also, Elior just sounds stupid."

Farrah turns around in what would've been a very dramatic exit if she had not bumped into a slender young woman and her dog walking down the street.

The woman regains her balance gracefully, but Farrah is so startled that her skin tone changes a few hues lighter before settling back into her chosen light honey tone.

"Madam, are you all right?" I ask and extend my arm to settle Farrah.

The woman is concentrating on her spilled drink and getting control of her chunky dog, whose walk has been rattled by the sudden towering of two people.

"No," she says in a monotone, raspy voice. "You spilled my iced coffee, and you got Grimace all riled up. Pay attention to what you're doing. Not everyone is as forgiving as I am."

She adjusts her hat and jacket before she continues walking a few steps and turns to the door Farrah had knocked on just a few moments ago.

Farrah and I look at each other and scream in unison, "Wait!"

The woman turns around with what I imagine is a scowl behind her sunglasses.

"What?" explodes out of her mouth as if offering a challenge.

I take the lead as Farrah is the equivalent to her spilled drink now.

"I think we are looking for you."

"You think, or you know?"

"I am not sure. A friend ...," I couldn't very well call Ms. Jessica a friend after my presence in her shop had betrayed her life, but it seemed disrespectful to treat her as a stranger when her reluctant kindness saved my life. "An associate sent us to this address. We are looking for a seer."

"I'm not a seer."

The young woman turns her attention back to her keys and opening the door.

"That's very interesting," Farrah interjects. "*Seer* is not such a common term, and any other person would've asked for clarification. Yet, you knew what he was asking immediately. Now, I'm not saying you're a seer, but you're probably the person we're looking for."

Just like that, my stomach drops again. If Farrah is right, Ms. Jessica has led us to a dark magic wielder—albeit one in shorts and strappy sandals.

The young woman groans and leans on the door to open it with her body weight.

"I don't take walk-ins, sweetie," she says to Farrah with a forced smile. "Let alone for hipster couples who don't even know what I do."

"Listen, *sweetie*," Farrah says without a misstep. "This man is not a man or my boyfriend, he's a fairy, and we need your assistance."

"First of all, that's an incredibly offensive and bigoted term. And second of all," the woman takes another look at me, "I really don't care. Goodbye now."

The woman closes the door on us, and Farrah goes up to it and yells.

"We're not leaving until you give us a chance to explain."

I run up to Farrah to stop her from attracting unwanted attention, and the door opens.

"Were you just going to ram my door?" the woman asks as if it was the most boring of choices.

"I, uh, no! I was just trying to get my friend here to stop shouting. We will be on our way now."

Farrah looks aghast, and I resign myself to finding help elsewhere. I am gaining some reconnection to the earth and can shift energy a bit more. So, maybe my memory will return in time and relying on a dark magic wielder would be unnecessary after all.

"You," the woman says with a blank expression. "The girl wasn't mocking you earlier, was she? You're not human."

"Can you sense such things?" I ask and stand in front of Farrah out of fear that this woman will unleash an attack.

"No," now she's annoyed. "Your shit lifted up when you ran, and I saw what looks like insect wings on your stomach."

The blood rushes to my face so fast that I almost think my nose will bleed.

"Come in. You have thirty minutes before my next appointment of the day."

We go up one flight of narrow stairs to the woman's apartment—which explains why no one responded to Farrah's knock. It's a large building divided into individual homes. This one in particular faces the street we were just standing on and is not what I expected from a dark magic wielder.

The large square has a bed in a corner where Grimace plops himself down. The room otherwise feels like a small common area. It's decorated with fluffy white rugs, gold and rose-pink accents scattered through the area, mingling with potted plants, which appear healthy and happy.

"We'll just cut right to the chase—" Farrah starts, but all her might and enthusiasm is stopped by the woman's single index finger being held in the air.

"You've been nothing but rude. I want to hear from the fae," the woman says, without turning her gaze to Farrah, and fixating on me as she takes a seat on a comfortable looking couch.

I look at Farrah and try to project calm with my eyes. She knows how to move in the human realm, but I know diplomacy. It's time to put my skills to the test, even if with a savage being.

"Thank you for having us, madam," I say and bow my head. "My name is Elior, and this is my companion, Farrah."

I give her a chance to introduce herself, but the woman remains silent with a blank expression on her face that neither reassures nor dissuades me from continuing.

"Um … we are here because, as you correctly assert, I am fae, but I have suffered memory loss, and I need to find my way back to my realm."

The woman crosses her legs and leans forward. "And what do you propose I do?"

"I … I am not really sure. I figured a dark—I mean, a seer would be able to see into my recent past and tell me where I traveled to this realm from."

"Speak your truth and be upfront. I've been told the stories. I know your kind calls mine 'dark magic wielders,' when you don't even understand what we do."

The woman speaks as if she has the higher moral ground. Just because she can help us does not mean she can forget her place in this world or any realm.

"You can imagine the struggle it is then, to be here and in need of your assistance," I quip as politely as I can.

"You come to my home—my place of business—demand assistance you can't name and think me inferior."

At this point, the woman's stoic face turns to a smirk. "The coffee was $4.75. You can leave the cash by the door. Please see yourselves out."

I bite my lips and unconsciously stand to a fighting stance. Grimace growls from the bed but does not get up.

Farrah rolls her eyes, and sternly tells me to sit.

"His wings," Farrah interjects. "He thinks his wings might guide him home, but he can't seem to expand them. Could you either use your magic to return his memory from the past few days, or strengthen his connection to the earth, or some crap like that?"

The woman turns to Farrah with a stoic look again. "There are spells for that."

I lower my guard. Grimace goes back to sleep. Farrah's eyes widen, and her smile is plastered on her face again.

"That's amazing!" Farrah says. "Can you help us?"

"Now, why would I help a fae?"

"He's got money."

"Does he now?" The woman's full smirk cracks her onyx complexion. "Is that why you're helping him? A creature from another realm has money that *you* can use in this one? My, you are as brilliant as you look."

My anger at being called a "creature" by a dark magic

wielder mixes with the feeling of dread over Farrah realizing this woman has a point.

But Farrah is in defensive mode as well. She paces behind the woman's couch, and by the time Farrah is in front of her, she changes to an identical replica.

"How smart do I look now?" Farrah says, in the woman's exact tone.

The smirk vanishes, and in its wake is left a frown. Farrah is getting to her.

"A changeling," the woman snarks. "Thought you were exterminated."

Another cup of dread is added to the cocktail of emotions inside me, and it's the overpowering feeling now.

"Please," I interrupt, standing in between the two replicas of themselves. "What can I offer you?"

All expression leaves her face once again, and the woman sits back.

"Finally, you're making sense." After a short pause, she adds, "Blood. From both of you."

I shift energy involuntarily, and a gust of wind comes from the window, strong enough to knock some items around the apartment.

"And you plan to do *what* with it exactly?"

"I don't owe you any explanation. That's my price," she says with finality.

I turn to Farrah, who has changed back to her previous form, ready to huff out of here in righteous anger, only to find a handsome grin plastered on her face.

"That's all?" Farrah says. "I've wasted so much currency on my kitchen floor, then."

Farrah spots my horrified face and puts the pieces of the puzzle back together. "Oh, calm down, Elior. What is she going to do with blood?"

"Magic," the woman and I say in unison.

Grimace breaks the tension by barking at the window.

"That must be my appointment. Please leave. You have my price and know where I live. Please make an appointment next time you decide to drop in."

Farrah looks pale. She didn't change her skin tone; she is scared.

"What's wrong, Farrah?"

"Her appointment," she says, looking out the window. "It's them."

CHAPTER 15

Conversations

My body shuts down due to the amount of feelings it's experiencing. Farrah paces around the small apartment while Grimace follows with his eyes, probably thinking he caused this shift in the room by barking.

"I need you to leave now," the woman says impatiently, standing by the door.

That is the only door. In and out. We would come face to face with the people trying to capture me and kill Farrah. How do they keep finding us?

"We cannot," I say in a low voice.

Considering my options of Farrah not knowing how to fight properly, and a pacifist fae with no staff for protection, the latter seems more appropriate.

"Do you know these people?" Farrah throws at the woman. "Are you working with them?"

The woman releases the doorknob and walks closer to Farrah.

"Listen carefully, dear. I work for myself, and I don't

owe anything to anyone. Now, what is going on, and who are these people coming to see me?"

The woman's stoic nature remains untouched through her line of questioning.

"We are not sure, but all day yesterday, they were trying to capture me by any means necessary. They shot Al—Farrah, and I think they killed the woman who gave us your address," the words falling out of my mouth are, once again, accompanied by numb tears.

The onyx slate once again slightly cracks. This time, the pursed mouth and furrowed brows make the cuts.

"And, you thought to bring them here?"

"They killed the woman who gave us your address, but she never told them that I was there. I do not know how they are tracking us, but we certainly have tried to evade and hide so as to not bring harm to anyone else."

Even the tears realize this is too much, and jump from my face to the ground, hoping for a reprieve from the pain.

"You don't know how you're being tracked in one of the most surveilled cities in the world?" the woman says in a huff, looking at Farrah.

A knock occurs on the door.

I look outside, and Lange and Shoto are down in the street.

"Shit," Farrah says to herself.

~~~

"Welcome, ladies," I hear the woman say to Varya and Eva, from behind the bathroom door.

While I crouch behind the door, Farrah extends her legs to stand over me and has her ear to the door, as well.
~~~

The woman's bathroom is compact but clean. An entire wall of mirrors force me to glance at myself. I am unrecognizable without my wings, regular clothes, or long hair.

The voices on the other side of the door are muffled, but we can still make out some things. It's easier to hear Varya's commanding voice and distinguish her accent from the other two. The other woman and Eva are soft-spoken, so we hear every other word.

"I don't think they came for us," Farrah whispers, worried.

The woman must've offered them tea because Varya says, "Just honey in mine."

There's too much silence. Enough to worry me. I want to tell Farrah to get ready to fight, but I'm afraid of not having the cover of the women's conversation to muffle my whisper. So, I just give her a disappointed look. She returns it with sad eyes and a sweet smile.

After a moment, I exhale loudly. I just heard the words "Lempara" and "destroyed."

My heart drops to my stomach. Is that what they're planning? To destroy my realm? This is exactly why my father prohibits us from crossing. If I make it back to him, we should seal the portals once and for all.

More silence.

I can only really hear Varya saying, "What's our best option?" and, "How would we manage to keep a portal open for that long?"

This does not bode well. Are they trying to use me to invade the fae realm and wreak havoc from within? How do they even know about it? What would they even gain from that? It's typical human destruction, and to be expected that they would turn to a dark magic wielder for help.

"May I use your bathroom?" Varya says clearly from the other room.

Farrah and I reach for each other's hand to hold, bracing for what happens next.

Nothing.

We hear the door to the hallway creak and slam shut. After some shuffling, the woman opens the door to her bathroom to find a nearly invisible changeling holding hands with a fae in fighting stance.

"So, what was that about?" Farrah asks the woman for both of us, not lowering her guard. But the woman waves us out and assures that the visitors have left.

We go back to the living space. I sit down on a chair, with my head between my legs. Grimace sits by my feet, probably sensing I'm in distress and wanting to comfort me. Nothing makes sense.

"You didn't mention you were royalty, mister," the woman points to me while she leisurely paces the room. "Pleased to formally meet your acquaintance, Prince Elior of Lempara."

She revels in those words as if she had stumbled upon a secret treasure.

"That is not a secret. But I am curious as to why that information was shared with you by those women," I snap back.

"They're looking for you. But I guess you figured that one out yourself."

"What did they want?" Farrah interjects.

"They're interested in what your friend can do for them. They want him to open a portal to his realm," the woman says to Farrah.

"And you didn't give us up because ...?"

"For one thing, I haven't heard your response to my proposition. And were you to accept my condition to help you, that would be a conflict of interest between my clients. I take that very seriously," the woman says, feigning disgust. "Besides, they weren't really clear on why they wanted you to open the portal. So, I don't really trust them."

"You agree to help us, and you can have my blood. As much as you want," I respond.

The situation has escalated, and now my entire realm in danger, not just myself. Whether this is a dark magic wielder or not, my hands are tied, and I need to act on behalf of my people. I rather have her helping me than them.

"Now, what did they ask, and what did you tell them?"

"Are you on board, as well, changeling?" the woman interrupts me and turns to Farrah.

A moment of hesitation from Farrah feels like a dagger in my heart, but she ultimately nods.

"Great to be in business together. You can call me Tenneh," the woman finally forces a proper smile.

~~~

After a round of tea, Tenneh explains that Eva had made an appointment with her a few days prior, saying she needed a real witch for what she was looking for. Tenneh also makes it clear that she prefers the term *witch* over dark magic wielder, for some reason.

Tenneh asks me the usual questions—what's the last
~~~

thing I remember and where I was when I woke up. I recite the answers like a chant because I've repeatedly asked myself the same things.

Farrah, bored of repeatedly hearing the same things she knows is lazily playing catch with Grimace. Neither of them seems very into the activity but glad to have some company.

"Where were you last?" Tenneh throws the question to the room just to fill the silence while she researches an old book of hers.

While innocuous, the question makes me realize something.

"I was in the human realm," doubt creeps into my voice.

Tenneh stops reading. Farrah continues haphazardly throwing the ball.

"But you remember your father pointing his staff at you, right?" Tenneh says, connecting the same dots I just did. "Why would he step foot in this realm?"

"Looking for me? I am not sure," I say.

"This one time, one of my mom's boyfriends asked me to come with him to a racing track," Farrah starts, recounting from the corner of the floor she's sitting in. "I must've been like fourteen or so. Anyway, I thought he just wanted to bond with me because I usually didn't get along with my mom's partners. Throughout the races, he kept taking bathroom breaks, which I thought was odd. During one of those breaks, I texted my mom to tell her I was going to ditch him and meet up with my friends instead. She replied, saying that I needed to stay and do whatever this man asked. Odd. But it tracked with her."

At this point, Tenneh and I are profoundly confused as to what's going on or the point of Farrah's story.

"As the final race started," she continued, "he came back and asked me to go with him for a second. After an entire day of mostly sitting by myself, I kind of just wanted to see the final race, you know? But I went with him, anyway, thinking I would be severely disappointed with either outcome. He takes me to an isolated corner, shows me a picture of a man, and asks me to change into that man. He said he just needed me to walk next to him to a group of people. And I did. Next thing I know, a group of five men escort me behind a booth and start beating me up and asking for someone's money. My mom's boyfriend leaves the tracks, and after the men were done, they left me there alone. After I made it back home, he was sitting with my mom, watching TV as if nothing had happened. You see, he needed money and knew these men were looking for the guy he had me change into, so he got a finder's fee while I got beat up by five men. I was so angry I lunged to attack him, but my mom interfered, saying he really needed the money and that I heal fast, and he made sure they wouldn't kill me."

"By God, that's dark," Tenneh remarks. "What the hell was that about?"

"Sometimes parents do bad things because they think you can handle it," Farrah says and throws the ball to Grimace again. "And sometimes they're just bad people. Nothing you've told me about your dad seems to make sense to me, and I'm not sure he doesn't play a part in you not having your memory. I've told you this, Elior."

Part of me knows that what Farrah is saying makes

sense, but I also know my father. He is kind and just and abides by fae tenants.

"If you really thought that was true, why would you stick around and help me knowing that your repayment depends on him?" I bark at her.

I immediately regret it.

Farrah drops the ball, changes into Matt's form, and gets up from the floor.

"You are completely right, Prince Elior," Matt says. This is the first time I've seen him—or any of Alex's forms—angry. "Why would I, indeed?"

He storms out of Tenneh's apartment, and Grimace lets out a small whimper.

"What the hell was that about?" Tenneh says, perplexed.

CHAPTER 16

Waiting

Two days have passed since Alex stormed out of Tenneh's apartment, and I've managed to contain my brooding to the floor in front of the window, as a form of subconscious punishment to be looking outside but being trapped with a witch.

I have no way of communicating with Alex to apologize. I feel like I ripped out my own heart. Why would I even question why she was helping me? I can't possibly cross realms without making things right with Alex first.

In the meantime, Tenneh has been making different concoctions to return my memory, but she refuses to tell me what's in them. I think she doesn't want my judgment of her magic, and it probably has components of living beings. We've gotten to an unspoken understanding to not discuss processes with each other.

The past two days have been mostly silent. I hide in the bathroom for long parts of the day while she greets clients. Sometimes, I bring Grimace or one of Tenneh's books with me to have some company to differ it from the times she's in there with me with a needle drawing my blood.

"We've been at this memory game for two days, and we're getting nowhere," Tenneh volunteers. "I think it's time we follow Farrah's instinct and work on your wings. Maybe we can make more headway there."

I know she's not doing it on purpose, but the mention of Farrah rips at my heartstrings again. And then, the tears come.

"You really have to stop crying. It's making Grimace and I uncomfortable."

"I think I hurt her feelings," I muster through the tears. "I do not like that she is out there thinking I do not care about her or that the bond we had in such a short time meant nothing to me."

"Elior," Tenneh says calmly, as she squats next to the chair I'm sitting on. "I really don't care about your love affair with the changeling. What I do care about is you making yourself useful and tell me how the hell to help you, sweetie, because my patience is wearing thin, OK? Great."

There's a knock on the door before I can reply to her passive aggressiveness with my own. Tenneh mentions she has no more appointments today, and from our time together, she does not strike me as the type of person who enjoys unannounced visits from friends.

Did Varya track me down here? She probably captured Alex and made her confess to my whereabouts. I let anger get the best of me, and now Alex might be paying the price for it. I sent them out there, directly into their arms.

I jump behind the couch in the tiny apartment and

Grimace follows me thinking, it's some sort of game. Tenneh goes to open the door slowly as she grabs something from the umbrella stand next to the door at the same time. It looks like a femur bone. Of course, a dark magic wielder would delight in using carnage as a weapon. Nevertheless, I follow suit and grab the nearest staff-like object near me to defend myself. I'm not having a repeat of the gym. As much as I dislike Tenneh, she has been helping me, and I should protect her and Grimace.

Tenneh finally opens the door, and I hear her the bone make contact with the door, and a deep male voice says, "Excuse me, miss. Are you Tenneh, the current resident of this apartment?"

"No," she says convincingly. "Who are you, and why are you looking for Tenneh?"

"I have some important information for her," the man says.

"You did not answer my question, sir. Please identify yourself before I start screaming bloody murder and call the police to report a home invasion."

Tenneh is fierce.

"You're so dramatic," the man says in a lighter tone. "You're literally the first person not to be charmed by this form."

Alex!

I spring up so fast from behind the couch that Grimace barks at me, startled. I take a look at Alex, and this is a form I haven't seen before. He is a tall, muscular, fair-skinned, and square-jaw man with bright green eyes.

"Huh," Tenneh mutters. "Thanks for giving yourself away, Farrah."

"It's Brett in this form, actually," he says. "What do you mean by that?"

"Your original form," Tenneh explains. "You were either born a man or a white woman—or raised by one. No black woman is charmed by a white man showing up at her doorstep unannounced."

Tenneh places the bone back into the umbrella stand and calmly returns to the small dining table/potion station.

I want to rush and give Brett a hug, but I'm not sure why he's back or how he feels about me.

"Sup, Tinker Bell," he smiles in my direction. And I take it as a cue that I'm forgiven and rush him.

Brett is taller than me, so my head only reaches his chest, but I squeeze as hard as I can and keep apologizing.

"Chill, man. I'm not mad at you," he says. "I actually came back because I figured out something that might help. Also, I made a lot of money."

When Tenneh comes back with three teas, Brett and I hesitate to even touch the cup out of fear she might've mixed some leaves with potion herbs.

She only has to raise one eyebrow for us to fall in line and graciously grab our cups.

"After I stormed out in spectacular fashion," Brett explains, "I thought I should treat myself to a nice day. And what better way to have fun with no money in Manhattan than being an attractive white guy? I was getting stopped in the street, people were whistling. Being catcalled as a man is a completely different experience, let me tell you. But I digress, the point is that first night, I ended up in a swanky apartment uptown overlooking the park. And the moon looked so beautiful, I wanted to take a picture with the park and the moon in it, and that's when it happened."

Tenneh has not looked up from her book during Brett's story. Impatient for the ending, I just open my eyes wider to him.

"You see, because I was taking a photo from behind a glass window when I pointed the camera at the moon, it created this weird halo around it, and it reminded me of the superlong story you told me about how your realm was created under a full moon! Maybe you need a full moon to remember and open the portal."

"That is not a terrible idea, Brett," I smile, trying to be endearing and dismissive at the same time, which just comes out as a neutral tone.

With the aloof attitude Brett has, I am ready to balk at his idea, but this is a solid lead. The fae revere the moon as a great cleanser and equalizer—a master that shines a light in the darkness and keeps the waters in balance.

Brett is odd. I know it's still Alex, and I'm so happy to see him back. This disguise brings out yet another different part of her.

Smugness is the closest thing to it.

I feel myself wanting to be better than him and wanting to be him at the same time. It's infuriating and just makes me resent him, but I want to have him around.

"You could have come back sooner then," I say loud enough for Brett to hear me but not take it as a direct question.

"Not quite, young grasshopper. There's more to this story," Brett interjects, laying down on Tenneh's couch. "For I had a job. The group of people I ended up hanging out with work at a gallery that was having a show yesterday. They asked if I could come by the next day and flirt a little with the guests, get them to drink more and buy more. While I was one step away from soliciting, it did give me a chance to make stuff up about art—"

"You are unbearable. Get. To. The point," Tenneh commands from the table.

"I'm almost there! Geez," Brett is not fazed by Tenneh's rude comment. "As I was saying, I was crafting grand stories of knowing the artist of a piece and how disconnected it was from reality, but I was telling this *to* the actual artist. She let me finish and then told me, 'It's not my nature to reflect reality. It's my duty as an artist to expand the possibilities of what the world could be if we can come together to make it a reality.' Boom!"

Brett is pleased with his story. I think he really believes he blew our minds. Tenneh keeps fiddling with ingredients and reading her book at the table, and I sit there for a few seconds just trying to figure out what that story had to do with me or getting back to my realm. Only Grimace is giving Brett the attention he was looking for and runs around in a circle. But I think he just wants someone to play with him.

"Boom what?" I finally ask.

"Boom, that's the key, man! You can't open the portal by yourself I don't think. You said the fae abide by the tenets of life, spirit, and balance. How are you to open a portal during the day by yourself? You either need more fae or the next best thing," he points at himself with the same smugness that makes me want to punch and hug him at the same time.

"The fact that you're making sense right now is honestly upsetting," Tenneh says without looking up. "What makes you think you're so useful?"

"Because changelings are the closest thing to fae in this realm," I interject, mostly to myself.

"So, the next full moon, you two hold hands, you recover your memory and then the portal appears? Got it," Tenneh's sarcasm is not appreciated, but the intent is taken.

Everything Brett connected was from the information I've told him before. I'm annoyed that he made the connections before I could, but that's when it hits me.

"No, I do not think I will recover my memory, because I do not think I lost it in the first place. I think information is being actively blocked."

CHAPTER 17

Dinner

Tenneh is not happy that her research into memory spells was wasted, and she is taking it out on Brett and me. Mostly, I think she just doesn't like company, and I've been in her space for a few days now.

"You know what," Brett loudly announces to the room. "I think we've made a lot of progress today, and I think we deserve a treat. How about dinner? On me!"

"Did you forget we are being hunted?"

"Um, you and that Southern blonde form of mine are. Not Brett," he refers to himself in the third person, and it's obnoxious.

But as I think about it, it has been a few days since Eva, Varya, and the other goons have come around. It's odd. No one who is so intent on capturing someone, and is willing to murder to get them, just gives up out of the blue.

"Should we track *them* down and make sure they can't chase us anymore?" Brett adds, punching his right hand with his left fist.

Not the smartest idea, but chivalrous, nonetheless.

After a pause, Tenneh responds.

"I took care of it," she says hastily. "When they came here, I told them the bones said you were going upstate to commune with nature."

I'm confused as to why she would be annoyed by my presence then. "Why did you not say that before? I have not left your apartment out of fear of being found."

"It doesn't matter. Your little friend is working with a hired group, and I'm sure they have eyes everywhere."

"Can't you do some magic so that we can go out together, and he's not recognized?" Brett asks Tenneh with a smile and the genuine innocence of a toddler.

Tenneh thinks about it for a second and checks her pantry.

"Yes, I can," she says. "I can brew a glamour draft for the prince here, and you two can go on your date."

My entire body tenses up. I do not want to make a movement or even the slightest sound. I want to hear whatever comes next out of Brett's mouth as his direct response to us supposedly going on a date.

"We are not going anywhere without you, Ms. Tenneh," Brett shoots back. "You have been a gracious host, and Elior would like to thank you, through me. I'm not taking no for an answer."

Tenneh's eyeroll speaks a thousand words. But Brett, now pleading with Grimace in his arms, makes a counter-effort.

"Fine. Give me an hour for the glamour and another to get ready," she relents.

~~~
~~~

Walking to dinner is a rush of emotions. I still see myself as *myself,* but after drinking the glamour draft, Tenneh said onlookers would not recognize my form as the one I see. I dared not ask Tenneh what she used in her brew, but it tasted of mercury mixed with cinnamon, which I suspect she added only for taste.

I must admit Tenneh looks beautiful … for a witch. She ditched the shorts and string-strapped blouse for a form-fitting, short, sky-blue dress with some ruffles at the hemline that match the shoulder straps.

Not to be outdone, Brett opts for a trimmed beard that accentuates his jawline, copper pants, and a white buttoned shirt with the sleeves rolled up to his elbows. Once again, I'm uncomfortable with how good he looks.

Brett is walking ahead, leading Tenneh and me, but after a few blocks, he points to a restaurant.

"This looks nice, we should eat here."

It's hard to tell with this form when he's asking or demanding something. We walk in, and all the seats in the vestibule are occupied by nicely dressed people waiting.

"Hi, beautiful. Do you have a table for three?" Brett asks the hostess behind a podium.

"I'm sorry. It's a two-hour wait for a table if you don't have a reservation," the hostess stammers.

Brett rests both forearms on the lectern and leans into the hostess. He towers over this short brunette girl.

"Are you sure there's nothing you can do for me, love?" he pleads with sad eyes paired with a smirk.

"I—I think I can help you," the hostess replies with a

big smile and red face, as she tucks her long hair behind one ear.

She slowly walks the three of us to a table in the back, lit by three small candles of varying sizes and heavily cushioned chairs, different from the ones we passed.

"I hope you have a good time, and please let me know if there's anything I can do to ensure that," the hostess says and returns to her post.

Good riddance.

"That was so gross," Tenneh kicks off the conversation.

"You have to use your talents to your advantage. And I guess I'm just naturally charming. Why are *you* so quiet?" Brett throws my way.

"It is interesting going to a banquet hall and having someone else take the reins of the evening is all," I counter.

Tenneh lets out a laugh, which is something rare for her.

"You're jealous because you're in a situation where your title or good looks can't aid you?" she retorts. "You two are so predictable."

Brett and I lock eyes, confused.

"How would you have me act, Ms. Tenneh? What is the proper etiquette for a foreign prince?" I calmly pitch the question.

What feels foreign is the word *prince* in my mouth. I rarely refer to my title; it's always just known.

"Not sure, but not hiding behind your title or looks is a good start," she hits back.

We're interrupted by a server asking for our order, so I just ask for the same things Brett does.

"Why don't you tell us a little bit about yourself, Tenneh?" Brett breaks the tension.

"I'd rather not," she quickly shuts him down.

The silence is awkward and uncomfortable. The kind of silence that only comes from three people out to dinner who are only interacting because they each want something out of the other. Brett miscalculated this one.

"There is this game we play during banquets with new guests at Lempara," I state, finally breaking the awkward silence. I can't take the stressful energy between the three of us. "To begin, the person to your left says a quality they admire about anything. Then you tell a story of the last time you had to describe something with that quality."

Tenneh just blinks very slowly in response, and Brett crosses his arms and leans back in his chair.

"That is the saddest game ever, Tinker Bell," Brett finally laughs. "I thought the fae were more dazzling than that!"

His comment draws a chuckle out of Tenneh and puts her at ease.

"It *is* silly, but we are doing it," I smile back at them, having just made up the ritual on the spot. "I will start. Tenneh, you have to give me a quality you admire."

"Respect," she says, eyes locked on mine.

The game can be lighthearted, or it can be a strategic way to get information. And Tenneh figured out the latter quickly. Game on.

"Respect, hmm," I think about it for a second, and it comes to me. "Last time, I had to describe something with that quality—from what I remember—was when I watched my father welcome a group of merfolk to Lempara. You see, our realm welcomes those who are part of the balance of nature but have been hunted or greatly affected by humans. When a being or a group is in need, my father will welcome them and provide a space for the asylum seekers to set up and flourish. My mother and sisters are then tasked with making sure the surrounding nature and other living beings are working in balance with the newcomers and the spirits.

"The last time our kingdom welcomed a new group, I was in awe of how respectful to their needs and culture my father was. He and the council worked to expand Lempara's ocean just a bit more to delineate a space for the new tribe, who had different customs than the existing tribes in our ocean. Then I came in as a cultural ambassador to explain fae tenets, culture, and responsibilities needed of them for the prosperity and respect of our realm. That's the last time I saw respect exemplified."

I'm sure this is new information for them both, so I am expecting some questions of fae practice.

"So, you segregate and indoctrinate? Got it." Tenneh says and takes a sip from the drink the waiter brought while I was talking.

"What? No. It is not like that," I immediately protest. She has no right to be so flippant about matters she knows nothing about and a realm she has never visited—or could ever visit. "We are respectful of life and strive for balance while taking care of the spirit. Those are the tenets I live by, and the ones that have kept our realm safe and prosperous. You don't know what you're talking about, with all due *respect*."

Sensing the growing tension at the table, Brett leans forward to grab his drink and raises it.

"Thank you for sharing your story, Tinker Bell," he says with a raised glass. "I humbly request his majesty for the next word."

He can be annoying, but the guy knows how to take control of the room.

"Uh, how about loyalty," I say with a raised glass between Brett and Tenneh.

"Loyalty! A classic one," Brett jokes. "Let's see, the last time I saw loyalty was …"

Brett stops, and his smile fades.

"OK, here's a story about loyalty," he says with a grim voice and a plastered smile, taking another swig of his drink. "I grew up with my mother, who had me very young. Most of her life, she just went from man to man, thinking the next one would be the one to solve all her problems. I guess that's how she met my father. A promising candidate who also left her as soon as he learned she was pregnant with me. He wasn't like me, you see, but one of his parents was, and he was afraid I would turn out like them. And I guess he was right to run away because I turned out to be his worst fear. After him, my mother became completely unhinged and chose progressively worse men. Anyone who would give her a modicum of attention was immediately a suitable candidate. Most of them would ignore me."

Tenneh and I can do nothing else but keep drinking.

"But they weren't all awful; one even taught me how to drive a motorcycle," he continues. "He was my favorite. During those times, my mom was better. She was caring and pushed me to do better in school and taught me different life skills. But there was this one guy she dated who learned of what I could do, and his relationship with my mother became dependent on my obedience to his plans. This was the guy from the racehorse track story.

"Anyway, he would come up with these plans on how to scam or rob people, with me pretending to be different people. Nothing too elaborate. But if I disagreed with anything, he would get so mad he would take it out on my mother. This went on for about five years. My mom knew he would only stay for what I could do for him, but she thought that was better than just us two fending for ourselves. He came up with different plans on how to make money. Up until then, we were just doing small hits to not raise suspicion and have a steady stream of income. Always the genius that he was. As I got older, he became afraid I would leave, so he ensured that he readied his retirement. That most recent plan was one of his biggest."

I'm drawing a blank, and for once since I woke up in this realm, I am focused on nothing else but Brett's story. Another gulp of my drink, and this time it doesn't make my face recoil from how strong it is.

"I was to pick up this rich developer's daughter from school by changing into her mother, so we could essentially kidnap the child," Brett continues with the ease of a natural storyteller. "Then, I would pretend to be the child and control the videos we would send to the developer. He said the child would be safe. And because I would pretend to be her mother, that she would never be able to point to us as culprits. We would request a couple million in cash that

I would then pick up by disguising myself, and the child would be returned a few weeks later. I reluctantly agreed to the plan, with the condition that the child's safety was nonnegotiable. He agreed. On the day of the kidnapping, I saw him pack a rope and what I later found out to be laced with acid. I backed out of the plan right then and there. I don't think he intended to keep the child safe."

This is the type of person I knew in my heart Alex was. An honest person who may be a little rough around the edges but ultimately believes in honoring life.

Tenneh continues to be quiet but, like me, seems enthralled in the story. Although I suspect that she would deny it, were she to be asked about it later.

"We got into a huge argument, and he threatened to throw the acid on me so I couldn't use my abilities anymore," Brett says with a small shake in his voice. "And he did. It didn't work, though. Obviously, I can change at will. But he did scar my original form. My mother heard us arguing, and she got to the garage as he was throwing acid on me. She was furious and pushed him to the ground. He got up and turned around to throw the rest of the acid on her and I don't know what came over me, but my arm turned into a spear shape and … impaled him."

Brett took a moment. With all the clatter in the restaurant, you could still hear the silence between Tenneh and me. Both of us afraid to make a sound or move.

The waiter returns and asks if we'd like to hear the chef's special. I stop listening after he says the word *filet*. In a hurry to get back to Brett's story, Tenneh turns to the waiter and says she would love it if he could just bring three of those and make mine vegan-friendly.

"Anyway," he continues, drawing a small smile on his face. "I just grabbed my jacket and my motorcycle and started driving north without looking back. After a few weeks of driving, I came to New York and decided it was as good a place as any to start a new life. I figured with how crowded it is here, that I could blend in and people wouldn't ask too many questions. But that's when I almost ran over Tinker Bell over here."

Brett turns to me and grabs my right hand on the table. "When you asked me to help you and offered to repay me, I saw it as a job. It was my chance to earn my money and do something good for once. I took it seriously, Elior."

This is the first time I've seen Brett—Alex—be so earnest.

"I know you chose the word *loyalty* because you felt abandoned when I stormed out. I know what abandonment is, and I would never do that to someone I made a commitment to. I will help you return home."

I'm horrified. The whiplash from Brett's story to what he just said to me gives me a headache. Or maybe it's the drinks? At the same time, his confession makes me feel secure. It's a similar feeling to falling from the sky and extending your wings at the last possible moment to not hit the ground. And that's what hanging out with Alex feels like. Not knowing if you're going to hit the ground at any moment.

I want to get up and kiss him. Or maybe that's the

drinks, too? I look over to Tenneh, who has not moved a muscle since Brett started talking, and I contain myself.

"I am sorry I doubted your commitment," I say, looking directly into Brett's eyes. "It has been a disorienting few days, and I latched on to you and unfairly placed an incredible amount of pressure."

"Don't get all sappy and serious. Gross," he says to me and winks.

In a flash, I remember what he just confessed to. And I slip my hand back to myself.

"Can we just go back to that story for a second?" Tenneh asks, frowning. "I have several questions."

"No," Brett responds through a laugh. "Trust."

"Trust what?"

"Trust. That's the word I'm giving you."

Brett draws a line in the proverbial sand. That was all he would share at this moment. Tenneh sits back and returns herself to her natural stoic state.

She looks at both Brett and me and then around the restaurant. As if her talking for more than three sentences would unleash unspeakable horrors in the room.

For all I know, that could be the case with a witch.

"Trust it is, then," Tenneh says slyly. A bizarre change. "The last time I had to describe something as trustworthy was myself. When I chose to not give you up to the people trying to find you—"

"Oh, come on, now," Brett interrupts. His tone is jovial, but his face is that of an investigator trying to figure out Tenneh. "You can do better than that. Elior and I told some stories to explain our examples. Take us on a journey, Tee."

The waiter comes back with two other servers to set the table for our meal. He removes the bread on the table that none of us even looked at and replaces our drinks. We all sit back and place our hands to our sides. Tenneh smiles at Brett.

"You want a journey, eh?" She says. "I can play along."

I'm not sure if the drinks Tenneh is ordering are having some sort of effect on her, or she just likes to be subversive toward Brett, but she tilts her head to let her raven braids fall to the side and expose her neck more clearly.

"Let's see, where to begin," she stretches both arms up. "I was born in Anguilla to a very poor but loving family. Nevertheless, my parents wanted better for me, so they sent me to New York to live with my aunt when I was nine. They trusted her to take care of me as her own. And she did … in her own way. My aunt was a single black woman in a foreign land. She learned how to survive here by using what she learned on the island. Santería—"

"Dark magic," I interrupt.

"If you want to call it that, sure, Mr. Respect," she snaps back. "From a young age, she taught me everything she knew. Unfortunately, she wasn't as skilled as I needed, so I took it upon myself to learn more on my own. In my studies, I befriended a group of … fanatics, let's say. They claimed to be actual practitioners of magic, but really they were fans of the art and were amazed that I really had a talent for it. They would ask for help with spells and brews every so often, and I willingly helped because I finally felt understood and accepted in this land. I didn't have a lot of friends outside this group.

"Eventually, this one girl comes to me, asking for help on a sleeping brew. Her mother had recently experienced a miscarriage and was experiencing insomnia, she said. Eager to help put her suffering mother at ease, I not only helped her with the brew, but I also taught her how to do it herself."

The servers return with our food, and Tenneh is silent until the last one of the servers is gone.

"A week had passed since I last saw that girl, and I was curious as to how her mother was doing," she continues while taking the silverware and picking at the plate with it. "Our group would meet every week to hang out and learn from each other—mainly me teaching the others tricks and techniques. But at our next meeting, I was by myself. I was disappointed and hurt that I was being excluded from the group, but then someone else showed up—a police detective. He walked over to me, with one of my vials in hand—the one I gave to the girl for her insomniac mother. He asked for my name and if the vial was mine, and I complied. He arrested me then and there. I was 16 years old at the time. He refused to explain what was going on until my parents would come to talk to him."

"Oh, Tenneh," Brett says empathetically.

Having learned from Brett's lesson, I keep quiet, holding my judgment for the end.

"They held me in a police station for more than six hours while my aunt finished her work shift," Tenneh continues. "When my aunt finally arrived at the police station, the detective told her that my friends had pointed to me as the one selling them the poison. My only friends here were lying about me and using me for their selfish games. Apparently, it had been going on for months. But it all came to a head when that girl used the sleeping brew to try to kill a classmate of hers. It then became a criminal case.

"That little white girl got off with a warning, and I faced adult charges. My aunt depleted her small savings to get me a lawyer and used her Santería to intervene. But there was another problem, and it was the fact that my parents never legally transferred guardianship to my aunt. So, in the eyes of the law, I was a runaway. Thus, they threw me into juvenile detention. That little group, and my time in detention, taught me how to be a quick judge of character. I know who to trust and who gives me pause.

"When you came to me asking for help," she points to me with her fork and takes a bite before the next word, "I knew you were pompous, with a self-righteous attitude only rivaled by your narcissism. But you mean well."

"You, on the other hand," Tenneh turns to Brett, "I couldn't pin down. But that little story of yours was something."

Brett's lips go from framing perfectly straight teeth to sealing his mouth shut. "You're going to sit there and judge—"

"No. I do not pass judgment," Tenneh quickly interrupts. "I actually respect and understand you better now."

I'm not sure whether Tenneh is being facetious or not. But it does concern me that I'm now trying to go back home with the aid of a dark magic wielder and a murdering changeling. I don't recognize myself anymore, and I'm not sure I should go back home after betraying myself and my teachings.

"This was a terrible game, Elior," Tenneh says. "But, I still got what I needed from it."

"So did I."

I lost count on how many drinks we've drunk, and they seem to be affecting everyone at the table. Tenneh is talking more loosely and flashing her smile more. Her body posture is also more open. I'm disconcerted that I also don't feel like myself, but knowing that her guard is down makes me drop mine. And I swear Brett just changed his form to appear more attractive.

An attractive murderer. How low have I fallen?

We enjoy a couple more drinks, and Tenneh and I even switch glasses to try each other's drink.

Brett asks if all banquets are like this in Lempara, and I have to let him down easy. He seems so interested in the fae realm now. It's cute and troubling. It also reminds me that this isn't my life. These two people do not fit into that, and I need to get back home and never speak of how I got there.

"I can't believe you called him a narcissist," Brett cackles to Tenneh. "I mean, you're not wrong, but I would've said 'conceited.'"

They both roar in laughter, and it does sting my ego a bit.

"I think I am pretty humble. I am not sure where this is coming from," I sense my words slurring a bit.

"Are you kidding?" Tenneh says in a louder tone than her usual sultry voice. "You've been sulking since I placed a glamour on you."

"True that," Brett agrees.

"Well, that is because I do not know what I look like really. I can still see myself as myself."

Tenneh and Brett look at each other and cackle once more.

"We don't know what you look like either, sis," Tenneh breaks through her laughing.

"What? What do you mean?"

"The glamour doesn't change your appearance. It makes you next to invisible. It's still you, but your appearance is blocked in people's memories. I'm looking at you right now, and I have no idea how to describe you."

Tenneh's explanation of her glamour is about the funniest thing she and Brett have ever heard. Their ruckus is starting to get on my nerves until I digest what she just said.

"Tenneh! The glamour," I interrupt the laughter. "Do you think the same principle could be applied to an entire day, or person, or both?"

The other two connect the same dots, albeit a little slower.

"I guess. But it would have to be powerful magic to make that kind of block and for it to last this long."

My dad would never be in the presence of a dark magic wielder. He would attack that person on the spot before sharing a space.

CHAPTER 18

Collision

Waking up on Tenneh's couch feels like I hit myself large tree trunk in the stomach right before opening my eyes. And it's clear I'm not alone with this feeling.

A groan originates from Tenneh's bed. Only she is sitting at her table with a steaming mug.

Did Brett sleep with Tenneh in her bed, or did he just move thereafter she was out? My stomach churns again.

Last night is coming back to me in bits and pieces. I think Tenneh killed someone, and Alex was unjustly arrested? A feeling of regurgitation starts from the pit of my stomach and swiftly climbs up to my throat. It was the other way around.

Must find my shirt. Pants are still on.

Tenneh drags herself from the table to me and hands me a mug. It's not steaming like hers.

"What is it?"

"Don't ask. Just drink it. It'll make you feel better."

"Did you two …" I glance at the lump that is Brett, covered by a thin sheet on her bed.

Tenneh rolls her eyes at me and walks over to him.

"Leslie, drink this."

Tenneh places a smaller glass cup with a golden thin liquid in Leslie's hand.

It takes me a minute to realize that this is Alex's other form, Leslie. She must've changed last night. I stop trying to cover my wings from what I thought was a stranger for a second.

"They're really something, aren't they," Tenneh says in a softer tone, referring to my wings, as she gazes on my shoulders while she walks back toward the couch I slept on.

"Yes. Albeit useless at the moment. It is as if they died hanging on to me."

Tenneh looks puzzled at my comment. The alcohol from last night couldn't have erased a fact she's known for days now. She knows my wings haven't expanded since I woke up in the park.

To be honest, I forget what flying feels like—another shameful admittance for when I go back home.

"Elior, I think you expanded your wings last night."

That can't be. I would remember something like that. Tenneh is being cruel right now and taking advantage of my memory lapses.

She reads the mapped emotion on my face because she says, "I'm not making it up. Ask Leslie when she decides to wake up."

"But, how? What happened?"

"I'm not sure. I think you legitimately blacked out during our walk back here and decided to climb a tree. Something about being the king of nature or whatever. Next thing we know, you took your shirt off, and we saw a faint glow through the leaves."

Wide awake now. Partly due to the drink Tenneh gave me, but mostly to her recounting of last night. I'm vastly more aware of my exposed torso.

"Did you actually see my wings?"

"No. The glamour was still working, but there was a glow, and the branches moved. And unless you have a glowing tail we don't know about, I'm pretty sure those were your wings," she says, pointing at my shoulder and abdomen.

I'm racking my brain to come up with an explanation as to how I could do that. But my brain turns back to the glamour. It is probably not in effect still, because Tenneh was pointing at my wings just seconds ago.

"The glamour, Tenneh," I say with urgency. "We talked about it last night, I remember. You said it could be a similar thing to what happened to my memory of the portal. Do you remember that?"

"I do," Leslie chimes in with a chipper attitude from her place on the bed. I'm glad for her confirmation, but I also can't stomach her presence right now. I'm already overwhelmed by the possibility of finding a way back home. I can't sort out my feelings over Leslie in the time it takes her to walk from the bed to the couch.

"Tenneh, the almighty and powerful sorceress, agreed that the logic presented by the king of the forest was solid, and thus, she shall take it as a framework for the next steps."

Leslie's grandiose attitude would be funny or charming had I not known that she is a runaway murderer. My gaze goes from Leslie to Tenneh, and from the corner of my eye, I spy Leslie deflate ever the slightest.

"Why would my wings contract to my body again?"

"Not entirely sure, but you got extremely upset when Brett changed form to resemble you saying he wanted to do a before and after photo as you with wings and no wings. You jumped down from the tree with them already back on your shoulders and told him that wasn't you anymore and started crying," Tenneh replies, uninterested in being the sole storyteller during this morning's performance.

"It was a fun night, though," Leslie interjects and sits next to me on the couch. "And productive!"

It slowly comes back to me. We did make a plan before leaving the restaurant. Brett and I discussed the next steps, which included visiting Central Park on the night of the next full moon and having Tenneh mix her magic with mine to awaken my wings.

"Are we sure about the plan? If what you are saying is right, it seems that I can expand my wings without help from your— um, magic."

While I don't want to offend Tenneh, I also don't want to involve myself further than I already have with her powers.

"Whoa, that's offensive," Leslie chimes in.

"You know what, let's settle this," Tenneh says, placing her mug down and sitting on the chair directly in front of the couch cross-legged and with a serene look on her face.

"What exactly makes you think your magic is superior to mine?" Tenneh inquires.

"We do not have to do this. I meant no disrespect. I just thought there could be an easier way."

"A way that doesn't involve my magic? I got that. But I insist, your majesty, what makes your magic superior to mine?"

Tenneh is not going to let up. She is being polite with her demeanor and sweet with her words, but they are honey-covered thorns.

"Very well, then. It stems from the simple fact that while fae 'magic,' as you call it, draws upon the spirit of the living and only redirects energy, your magic draws upon death and emotion."

The room falls silent. Even Grimace stops sniffing for crumbs by the kitchen floor. Did I go too far?

In reality, there's not much the fae have been able to learn about human dark magic wielders. Their powers, while we know started from mimicking ours, are a mystery to us.

Leslie's eyes dart between Tenneh's and mine. Tenneh stretches her neck to the side and back and gives a small smile.

"Your powers are reliant on other beings, while mine rely on myself and beings that already lived their lives. I'm not out here *shifting* the energy of beings other than my own."

"You see it that way because humans do not understand the balance between life and spirit. We do not rob any living being of anything, nor do we hold them hostage to our wills. We work together in harmony and ask of them what is best for us. They allow that energy shift because they know we will protect the balance that keeps them alive," I reply.

"Do you honestly think I kill living beings in order to perform my magic?"

Tenneh sits back, arms crossed, and her gaze unwavering from mine as if she expects me to attack at any moment.

"I do not know. But I do think it is in your interest if something were to die so you could use that energy."

The question she poses is nonsensical. While she may not resort to that level of magic, there's no denying that in times of war, they are capable of such tactic.

The tension in the room builds like water in a tea kettle, and Leslie is the whistle.

"I've only known both of you for a very short time, but all I've seen Tinker Bell do is lift some ground and blow some wind about," Leslie says. "And you, Tenneh, have mostly just been brewing teas. Neither of you has done anything egregious to do your little tricks. You'd think we're talking about actual magic."

In trying to defuse the situation, Leslie's whistle turns our attention to her.

In a swift motion, Tenneh gets off her seat, crouches down, mutters something under her breath, and turns to face Leslie, both hands holding large flames in the shape of blades.

The sudden display of raw power is mesmerizing and truly terrifying. Not only is she conjuring fire, but she's giving it a shape. She's being precise with her power; something not most of the fire-wielding fae can do. Tenneh is more dangerous and powerful than I give her credit for.

I take it as a cue to show Leslie what's at stake, but my connection to nature is still not strong enough to manifest fire. I concentrate on my surroundings and shift the energy from the moisture in the air to condensate it into my own two blades of water.

Leslie's face lights up with excitement. She starts laughing and applauding, which is disconcerting. Tenneh's fire extinguishes, and my water blades turn to puddles on the floor. Grimace comes over to lick them.

"You see, you just need a common goal. The way I see it, you are two sides of the same coin, and you're just mad because you've never seen the other side. And now that you do, it's not everything you built it up to be."

She is not completely wrong. My biggest fear meeting Tenneh was that she would instinctively work toward my demise. However, her actions have been nothing but kind, even if her attitude isn't.

"I do not think we will ever agree on how best to approach our powers. But I can give you my word that I will not harm or impose my will onto any being or spirit. All I ask is that you do the same, at least in my presence," I offer to Tenneh, kneeling on one leg.

"God, you're dramatic," Tenneh rolls her eyes with a smile. "But, I can agree to those terms."

I stand up, and Tenneh offers me her right hand. I grab her forearm and shake it in accordance.

"Isn't that sweet," Leslie fawns. "How about I send Matt to get us some breakfast?"

Food sounds perfect right now. Tenneh instructs Leslie to go to a nearby shop and gives her a small piece of paper with an order for the three of us and Grimace.

As Leslie walks to the door, she changes to Matt, pats

Grimace, and turns to give me a wink before walking out the door.

With the last click of the door closing, Tenneh comes over and asks what my issue is with Matt, Leslie, Brett … Alex.

A full day has yet to pass since learning that Alex was capable of an unforgivable act. So, it catches me by surprise that Tenneh can already see the turmoil in my mind as if it was plastered on my forehead.

"What do you mean?" I ask, feigning surprise.

"Not that I care, but if you're feeling some type of way toward her, you better bring it up quickly. In my experience, ignoring emotional issues only makes them grow faster."

"You do not understand. The first and most important thing we are taught as children is the value of life. Knowing that she is arrogant enough to make a decision as to who gets to live, and just continue with her life as if nothing happened, is unnerving."

"How do you know how she feels about it if you don't ask and talk to her? Don't let your judgment of her actions contextualize her feelings about it."

"There are some things you cannot walk back from. And now I know what she is capable of."

Tenneh just looks at me with a furrowed brow—not with judgment but concern.

"You're going to tell her what happened to the last of the changelings, then?" she asks.

~~~

Matt returns with two bags of food in hand. My heart mistakenly beats with excitement, but my mind is quick to
~~~

remind it to stop any sort of extra blood flow. My heart and my mind can pick up this battle another time because Matt came in as if he had gotten a glimpse of his next life.

"Did they pack the toast and the eggs in different boxes as I asked?" Tenneh asks, ignoring the obvious tension within Matt.

"Can you not see he clearly has something more important to say?" I say.

"Sure, but he's being all dramatic about it by not talking, and I'm hungry."

She's right, and I am hungry, too. I look back at Matt, who is now just leaning with his back against the door, bags still in hand.

I get up to grab the bags.

"They're here, and they saw me," Matt finally says before I grab the food.

I stop in my tracks. Tenneh looks confused and stands up from the kitchen table where she was tinkering with a brew.

"The people who are looking for you guys?" she asks.

"Yeah," Matt says with a defeated tone. "I was about to walk out of the cafe, when I spotted the big guy putting some metal boxes and a stack of car batteries in a van. I don't think he fully recognized me, but he definitely stared. I quickly walked away."

"So, that's why he came back so fast," Tenneh mutters to herself, not really caring about what Matt just said.

My nerves boil up to the surface and spill out of my mouth. "What if they know we have been here the whole time and have just been waiting for a good time to strike?"

"Because there's going to be a better time than the three of us inebriated?" Tenneh says, finally getting up and grabbing the bags from Matt's hands.

"I do not know, but it is unnerving that they are so close and clearly planning something. What do you think was in those boxes?" I ask Matt. "And what are car batteries used for?"

"To power a car," Matt says, almost in a mocking tone. "My best guess is that they know something about your kind and how skittish you are around electricity."

Humans, once again, prove that they know no bounds. They're trying to gang up on one fae with a cruel tactic.

My options are even narrower than before. These people are not going to stop until I leave this realm. Either I make it easy for them and leave Lempara without its crown prince, or I have a dark magic wielder help me fully connect with nature to defend myself.

"Tenneh," I say with contempt, knowing what I'm about to ask of her. "Can I offer you extracts from my wings in return for training in your approach? Other than my blood, which you already claimed, it is all I can offer right now. I desperately need to solidify my connection with nature again."

The request is shocking enough to stop Tenneh from further slathering her toast with what I can only assume is a mashed grapes.

"Sure," she says plainly, before turning her attention back to the toast.

I wasn't expecting her to be so willing to accept. At

the very least, I thought she would want to haggle on the payment.

"That's nice for you both, and I'm so happy you're getting along, but let's not forget they're trying to kill *me,* too," Matt protests. "And I don't know if you've noticed, but I can't do your little element blades."

But he can make his arm impale a living being.

"Have you ever changed to nonhuman forms?" Tenneh asks, with the simplicity one uses to ask about the weather. She doesn't even pause from eating her breakfast.

CHAPTER 19

Training

The next full moon is in three days, according to Alex's phone. In that time, I need to regain full connection with nature, unblock my memories of what happened to me, and consciously extend my wings in order to, hopefully, find a portal back home. No pressure.

Alex decides to take the blonde female-presenting form in which I met her. I hadn't noticed at the time the small freckles around her nose. She looks beautiful and finally introduces this form as Alana to Tenneh and me.

"I like this one," Tenneh admits. "She seems like she doesn't take crap from anyone."

"She does not," I instinctively say, and Alana darts back a playful look that just melts me.

No time for that. Or for her.

The three of us make our way up the stairs to the roof of Tenneh's building. She said it could be helpful to feel the wind and sun on my skin, without having to risk being spotted at a park.

To everyone's surprise, her neighbors have created some

sort of greenhouse area on the roof. My fae self is so excited to see humans put an effort to bring life and nurture it in an unlikely place.

Tenneh looks around confused. "This is … better than expected, I guess."

She turns to Alana and asks for her phone, to which Alana reluctantly complies. After typing something on the phone, Tenneh hands it back to Alana. She asks her to go between the tall planters to find some shade and practice turning just one arm into the different paws from big cats she searched for. She then turns her attention to me after telling Alana to not come out until she can do four different ones.

"Why don't you start by explaining what a connection to nature is, how it feels, and how is it different from the things you're already able to do?" Tenneh asks while sitting down on the roof cross-legged.

She traded her usual short pants and flowy shirt for some high-waisted, tight, stretchy pants and an accompanying chest covering. She said it was her "let's get to work outfit." And she meant it.

Growing up among fae, I have never had to explain what something that's inherently a part of us feels like. It takes me some time to even put it into words.

"There is this thing among a few species of trees, like eucalypt, black mangrove, and the sorts, where the crowns of fully grown trees do not touch each other, forming a sort of canopy. Much like an animal's skin pattern," I use an example that feels the closest to what my connection to nature feels like. "Essentially, trees of the same kin can sense each other's presence and be respectful of their own space to make sure there is room for the other.

"That is as close to what I can explain. When fully connected, I can feel myself in relation to living beings, the elements, and their spirits. Being aware of the space I occupy, and that of everyone else's, makes it natural to request movement of any of them. Of course, it does not work with living beings with willpower. So, while I can sense their presence in a space, I cannot move another fae's energy or a human's or animals for that matter."

Tenneh is not moving a muscle. She's thinking—but I can't tell about what because her large black sunglasses cover her almond-shaped eyes.

I realize that she's not speaking because she asked two questions, and I only gave a lengthy answer to the first.

"And I guess I can do minor things like lift loose ground or turn moisture in the air to water because I have been physically close to it when I have."

"Come sit down," she instructs. "What you're describing is a form of empathy extended to all things living and not, connected in harmony. But as you've seen for yourself, the human realm is not in balance. Our ozone layer is deteriorating, ice caps are melting, natural disasters keep getting stronger and stronger, and different species keep going extinct."

I follow her directions and sit cross-legged as well, in front of her. If this is meant to comfort me, she is failing.

"Here," Tenneh says, extending her hands.

Now holding hands under the afternoon sun just feels

awkward. She's not saying anything, and I'm not sure what she thinks this is accomplishing.

"You need to be quiet."

"I have not said anything."

"Your mind. It's cluttered, and you're so anxious it's transferring to me. Stop it."

"That is not very encouraging."

"It wasn't meant to be, your highness. It's an order, not a request."

Tenneh's remarks always teeter the line between rudeness and directness. Still, I figure that if she wants to be overtly rude, she will just be rude.

All right, calming the mind. I try to focus on my breathing and straighten my spine. I have to calm myself to focus on my breathing and relax, but the thought of having to do it quickly makes me more anxious. I have to breathe to stay calm, but the breathing is making me anxious.

Breathe in. Hold. Do it right. Breathe out. It's not fast enough. Repeat.

My palms are sweaty. Tenneh is going to know I'm not calm, which makes me even more anxious.

She sighs and squeezes my hands. Hard.

"Hold my hands. That's all you need to do."

I let my mind run wild while holding her hands. After a few minutes in silence holding hands, the thoughts calm down, and I can sense the rhythm of her breath.

We sit like that for a few more minutes. It's calmer when I close my eyes. Every so often, my mind goes on tangents, but it's fine. I bring my focus back again on Tenneh, her breathing, and now I can sense the flow of her energy.

She's keeping a lot of energy around her chest. I begin to wonder—

"That's enough," Tenneh pulls her hands from mine and stands up. She walks over to a table covered in what looks like empty pots, grabs one, and brings it back to me.

"Did you feel connected to me?" she asks.

"Yes. More than I thought I would."

"You're welcome. I opened myself up for that to happen, but you also had to be in a place where you allowed yourself to receive energy from me."

I must have been getting too close for comfort. Tenneh hands me the pot, and I see that a small sunflower is starting to bloom.

"Why did you give me this?"

"Because to grow and bloom, any being needs a lot of energy," she says matter-of-factly.

"I am not sure I can help it grow without touching it."

"I'm not asking you to do that. The way you talk about nature is how I connect with humans. Just connect with the flower and feel its energy. I can only do that with people, but do let me know if it works."

Tenneh walks off over to the area Alana is and walks between the bushes to check on her.

I can't really hear what they're saying, but raucous laughter breaks through, and my name is called.

As I walk over, I hear snickering … from Tenneh? It's the first time she has openly laughed around me—without the aid of alcohol. I push through the bushes to find Tenneh standing over a sad-eyed smiling Alana.

"What is happening?" I ask, immediately looking

down and spotting Alana's paw-like extremity coming off her shoulder. The most jarring aspect of the situation isn't that Alana probably did a historic thing by becoming the first changeling to change form to something other than human, but the fact that her arm/paw has no fur. It is a human flesh paw.

Looking pleased and embarrassed, Alana protests, "It's been like an hour, and I haven't done this before. Stop judging me!"

Her comment is in fake outrage, which only makes Tenneh laugh more. "I figured the fur would be the first thing you'd try!"

"No, you do structural work first and then build from there and add details," Alana explains, mostly as a reminder to herself.

Structural work—it's what Tenneh is trying to make me do with that flower. However, just like with Alana, she assumes how each of our abilities work stemming from her own. The basic structure for me isn't to feel the energy of a flower in a pot; it's a whole. Our tenet of balance implicates a totality of life. That small flower cannot grow without the water, air, and soil that feed it. I can't isolate beings because it's not in my nature to do so.

"I know what I have to do," I tell no one specifically.

I make a run for the door and walk a few flights of stairs back down to Tenneh's apartment. I open the door and head directly for Tenneh's closet. I try to find something, like a large garment with a hood. She has one in the very back. I trade my shirt for the jacket, and while it's a little short on me, it's not short enough to expose my lower wings that adhere to my back and abdomen.

As I throw the hood on, grab a pair of sunglasses, and head for the door, Tenneh, and Alana catch up with me.

"What the hell are you doing?" Alana yells out of breath, trying to change her paw back to an arm. "Where do you think you're going? You know those people looking for you are probably skulking around."

"I know, that's why I came to grab something to cover my face."

"And show your wings," Tenneh interjects, pointing at my now exposed lower abdomen. "You could've just kept the shirt underneath and put the hoodie on top of it."

"It is kind of hot outside, though," I say quietly.

"Well, he's not wrong," Alana reluctantly agrees.

Tenneh just stares at me, no sunglasses this time. Her signature stoic face is hard to ignore.

"I figured out what my structural work is. And I need to get to a park with a large green area or a body of water."

"Why?" Alana asks.

"Because the reason I have not felt connected to the earth since I woke up is that the balance in this realm is non-existent. You have greenery and some semblance of nature *in spite* of humans' behavior, not because you have allowed it to take place. I need to go below the battered exterior."

"What do you mean?" Alana seems more confused than usual.

"I need to be buried."

If Alana's eyes could pop out of her skull, they would've

jumped out from my statement. Tenneh's expression does not change, and her energy level remains unenthused.

"Can it wait until sundown, at least?" Tenneh simply asks.

"Fine."

CHAPTER 20

Connecting

Tenneh thought it would be a good idea to go to the Hudson River by the piers shrouded with a crowd and next to a body of water. She said we would leave only after she concocted a new glamour brew. In the meantime, Alana practiced animal forms on several limbs at a time—albeit furless for now. I continued trying to connect with the baby sunflower, which I did after a few seconds. So I just made my way around the roof, greeting all the plants and sensing their thirst for rain.

We left shortly after sunset, one at a time, so as not to walk out as a group. And this time, Tenneh made us all take a sip of the glamour brew.

It takes us a while to get to the pier, but Tenneh thought that if we were caught, it would be better to have it be in a place far away from her home and covered by a crowd.

I'm drenched in sweat from the walk and the nerves, but I remind myself that no one can actually remember what I look like right now. It helps somewhat. My mind is racing, capturing the faces of every person we pass on the streets.

I wonder where each of them is going to or coming from. Anything to distract myself from what I'm about to do.

"What is the plan now that we're here?" Alana asks. It's hard to tell her apart from Tenneh while they're both under the glamour's effects.

"Now, I find a heavy rock and dive in," I say, forcing a smile that will likely go unnoticed to them but helps assuage myself.

The plan seems simple enough. In theory, I should be able to have a stronger connection with the earth once I go past the surface.

"Let's say your reckless idea actually works and you get some sort of connection when you're down there. Wouldn't you just lose it when you come back up?" either Alana or Tenneh asks. I can't tell who due to the glamour potion.

"That is not how it works. I do not *have* to be touching the earth to feel connected to it, but I must do it to center myself and establish that connection … I think. I hope."

"How long can you stay underwater?" Tenneh asks. I can tell it's her who asked the question by the lack of enthusiasm or any other emotion in the tone.

I shrug. I'm not entirely sure. At my best, I can pull oxygen from the water and be able to pseudobreathe for some time, but in my current state I expect to last about the same as a regular human.

The three of us walk slowly toward the water, and I discreetly start picking up rocks and putting them in a bag Tenneh lent me. She said it would be less suspicious than hugging a big boulder.

We finally reach the waterfront, and the bag feels heavy

enough to pull me down even on dry land. I thought I would say a few words before diving in, but as I turn to the ladies, a man with a hat and flashlight is coming toward us short of jogging. The girls turn around, see him, get close to block his view of me, and one of them kicks back and pushes me into the water.

I can't really take a full breath before hitting the water, so I'm floundering and sinking. Maybe this was a bad idea. I was just going on a hunch, after all.

Too late now.

The air in my lungs is running out quickly, I'm sinking further and further, and I don't feel any connection to nature. My nerves start spiking again, and I wonder if I have enough oxygen in my system to get me to the surface. I hit the river bottom, but I can't see anything. It's pitch black. My mind is going a million different directions, and that's when Tenneh's face flashes in my mind. I know I have to stay calm as she instructed. It's harder to stay calm when you're running low on air, but I have to give it my best shot.

The cold dissipates, and I'm suddenly aware of the pressure of the water. I must be dying. My body instinctively gasps for air and, somehow … I'm able to fill my lungs.

I'm starting to feel … life. Flickering, but it's there.

I can see around me. There's a lot of trash down here, and an overwhelming feeling of pain overcomes me. It's not coming from anything internal. I'm feeling the river's pain. Hundreds and hundreds of years of abuse have left it numb to the pain that's new to me. In an act of gratitude, I shift energy to help the plant life grow and flourish and help its mother. The river get some respite, if only momentarily. But I know it's not enough.

As I make my way up to resurface, I'm able to feel every droplet of water, every wave I'm making, every plant, and every fish. I'm ecstatic to regain my connection with nature, yet it's a bittersweet connection. On one hand, I can feel this realm, and I feel strong in my ability. Yet on the other hand, I mostly feel its pain. This is not the same feeling I get in Lempara.

I emerge from the water, and my eyes take a second to adjust. We didn't think this through, and it's going to be hard for three people under the effects of a glamour to find each other if separated.

And that's when I see her. Eva.

She's walking hand-in-hand with a tall man, and I feel jealous. I can't explain why, but seeing the woman who has been trying to capture me and use me to break into my realm makes me feel possessive, and I want to confront her.

The water pushes me up to the pier and, once I step foot on it, I start running after them.

I'm just going on emotion. I feel protective over Eva, as if she was mine to keep from this man. My right arm is enveloped by a blue flame that flows down in the form of a whip. I'm just a few steps behind them now. I raise my arm to unleash my burning whip when I feel someone grab my left arm from behind. Instinctively, my body turns and raises a wall of rock from the ground to separate me from my attacker. It knocks the person back.

"What the hell, Elior?" she screams.

I subdue the flames and return the stone to the ground.

It is Alana … Alex? I'm not too sure with the glamour. People are starting to gather around us. We may not be recognizable, but I'm pretty sure humans aren't used to seeing fire whips or the ground ejecting upward. I come to my senses, pick up Alex from the ground, and hastily move past the crowd.

Thankfully, enough people gathered after I accidentally knocked Alex back that Eva didn't see me. And if she did, I'm relying on the glamour to hold its end of the bargain for the price of its ingestion.

Out of the way of people who are gathering, we make it past the piers and into the city blocks. Still wet from the river and sweat, Alex protests and releases herself from my arms.

"What was that little show back there?" Tenneh appears behind us with no glamour to hide her face. She's standing up straight with her left hand on her hip.

"How did you find us?"

"You think I would have us all wear glamours and not have a way to track you?" Tenneh asks as if it was obvious. "And it's nightfall, I can move through the shadows."

I'm not sure whether that last bit is meant as a joke or if she can actually move through shadows.

"I saw Eva."

"So did we!" Alex yells. "But, we didn't freak out like you did!"

Tenneh's tough facade breaks ever so slightly for a slight bit of worry to peek through.

"You clearly reconnected with whatever you needed to," she says to me with a stern tone. "Let's go back now before you decide to get us killed again."

CHAPTER 21

Memories

The walk to Tenneh's apartment was largely silent. Every so often Alana, now with the glamour worn off, tries to talk to me, but Tenneh huffs and sighs heavily, ensuring we know it isn't the time to discuss what happened.

Once we're back at the apartment, Tenneh lets me know that I am a "selfish jerk and could've placed all of us in danger." She goes over to her bed, skipping her usual nighttime routine, and turns off the lamp next to it.

She wants the day to be done. I follow suit and try to get comfortable on the couch. Alana walks over, before going to the makeshift bed on the floor next to Tenneh's bed and tells me, "Overall … I thought it was a fun night."

~~~

I'm the first one to wake up and realize what happened the night before needs an explanation that I am not sure I have. I sit up on the couch and look over to Tenneh's bedroom area and can spot her on her bed and Alana on the floor next to her.

Grimace notices I'm awake and comes over to demand
~~~

his ears be scratched. I can sense he's a little thirsty, so I turn some moisture in the air to water in my hand, and he drinks from my palm.

"You can give the dog water but can't be bothered to brew some coffee for us?" Alana says from the floor.

"I, um …"

"You don't know how to do that, I know, your highness," she says.

Her words are thrown with exasperation and softened with a smile. My heart is equally frozen and then provides an ember to thaw.

I head to the bathroom and splash some water on my face. I'm not entirely sure who the person is staring back in the mirror. Having feelings for a murderer, collaborating and living with a witch, almost attacking a human, feeling jealous over my hunter. This isn't me. I haven't seen my wings in so long, my hair is cut short, and I almost drowned myself to get something I have always innately had. I'm such a failure. I can't even go back home. The simplest things any fae can do, the prince is struggling with. I'm a disappointment to my people, my family, and myself.

Tears start falling down my face. My hands, gripping the sink on both sides, start trembling. My legs start buckling, and they lower me to the floor before completely giving out. The drama of the situation is not lost on me, but I also can't help it. I'm on the cold floor with my knees to my chest, and I'm sobbing. I can't stop, and all that keeps swirling in my mind is how much of a failure I am.

"Elior," I hear Alana knock on the door. "Are you OK?"

Why did I have to be so loud?

I calm my sobs into a cry. "Ye—Yes, I am fine. I will be out soon."

The effort to sound cheerful only cracks my voice further.

"OK, then," Alana responds after some silence. "I'm out here if you need anything."

Her shadow disappears from the foot of the door. My chest takes that as a cue to compress into itself. My lungs battle to keep it at bay, but my breath is not providing full assistance.

After what seems like an eternity but is probably a few minutes, the breathing returns to normal, and my tears stop falling. My legs regain some strength, and my hands stabilize. I'm able to pull myself up, not because I am done feeling bad for myself, but because I don't want Alana and Tenneh to have to ask me to use the bathroom.

I splash water on my face again, but this time I avoid the mirror and I walk out of the bathroom.

Tenneh and Matt are sitting in the living room with steaming mugs and a few pastries in front of them. Was this his way of distracting me?

"Do you want tea or coffee, Tinker Bell?" Matt asks with a smile and stands up to fetch either option I request.

"Chamomile tea would be nice. Thank you, Matt."

He gives me a reassuring smile as he turns to the kitchen.

I find a place to sit on the couch I was previously laying on and reach out to grab a pastry. The squared ones are usually filled with chocolate; those are my favorite.

Tenneh sees the one I'm reaching for and grabs it before I can, and holds it in the air, then offers it back to me.

Once again, her silence coupled with her stone-like face, commands answers without having to ask the question.

"I do not know what came over me," I simply say.

Matt comes back with some tea bags, honey, a small spoon, and a mug. Het sets all the materials on the table and pours steaming water from the pot they already had out. He's wearing a sleeveless shirt, which reveals a now more toned version of this form. Did he notice I liked the Brett form?

I explain what happened after I was pushed into the water. How I thought it was a mistake, and how eventually I could feel the pain of the river and felt connected again.

"That's all nice and fine, but when you went down, the security guard thought we were disposing of trash. And in a way, we were," Matt says, looking for a laugh that only Grimace returns with a yawn. "After that, we saw Eva walking with a guy, but they didn't seem to be on any sort of mission. It kind of looked like a date if you ask me."

My heart starts beating faster.

"Then, out of nowhere, we see someone with a freaking fire whip behind her," he continues. "Tenneh stayed back to do damage control, and I went to stop … whatever it was you were trying to do. Which was?"

"I am not really sure, to be honest. When I returned to the surface, Eva's was the first face that I saw, and it was like seeing an old friend. Then I saw she was with that man and I guess I wanted to protect her?"

"The guy who doesn't believe in violence and has been judgmental of those of us who resort to it?" Tenneh interjects, meaning to scold and sound superior. It must be a cosmic joke that she has the moral high ground at this particular moment.

"I did not do anything, really—"

"Because I stopped you," Matt interrupts, now visibly upset. "To my detriment, I should add. I still have a backache from when I hit the ground. But you were a man with a weapon stalking a small woman. If not for the matter that it would be tough to argue self-defense in that situation, but for the fact that you didn't know whether her little gang was around. It was a stupid move, and the first thing out of your mouth should've been a thank you to Tenneh and me."

He's right. Excusing my behavior by comparing it to their own transgressions does not grant them immunity; it's hypocritical. I should do better and recognize those who help me when I can't do it on my own. However unqualified they may be.

"You are right. I apologize, and I thank you both. Matt, or Alana, for stopping me from whatever was to come next, and Tenneh for—," my mind starts asking questions. "How *did* you manage the situation?"

"A few incantations can make a crowd believe what you tell them to believe. Plus, the glamours did some heavy lifting here," she calmly says before taking a bite out of the crescent-shaped pastry.

Her abilities continue to be a mystery, and she is reluctant to share even the slightest of details. But I guess now I know Tenneh's powers span from potions to summons to incantations.

"Well, thank you. I continue to be indebted to you," I say flatly.

"It's clear you know Eva," Matt says, still reeling back his animosity. "Or at least knew her before the memory stuff. Too bad you can't talk to her to figure out how you know each other."

That's actually a good idea. Maybe not talking to Eva herself, but talking to someone who might have met or seen both of us before I stopped remembering her. They might have some answers.

"I think I know how to talk to her, or about her, rather," I say, as I try to focus on the specifics, which leaves me probably looking absentmindedly at nothing. "I feel a stronger connection with nature, its spirit, and life now. If we can find the park that I woke up in again, I can try to sense who was with me prior."

Tenneh perks up and places her mug and half-eaten pastry down on the table.

"Are you sure about this?" she asks. "Is it worth risking exposure just to find out who this woman is, instead of focusing on getting you to the portal?"

She has a good point. Maybe this is just a waste of time. For all I know, my mind could be playing tricks on me, and Eva just looks like someone I know from my realm. She does have a similar facial structure that we all do.

After some pondering, Matt chimes in again. "I think that's a good idea. Clearly, Eva is out on dates and not focused on finding you. It's like they're waiting for something. And we still have two more nights for the full moon. So why not go do as much opposition research as possible, in case that wench is just biding her time?"

I do not care for the insult hurled at Eva, even if she *was* trying to kill Alex and me.

Annoyed at the situation, Tenneh gets up and addresses both Matt and me. "Very well, I'll go with Elior to the park, and you can stay here with Grimace and practice changing into a relative of his. We can't keep attracting more attention by going everywhere as a group."

We all agree to the plan, and I can finally eat the chocolate pastry.

CHAPTER 22

Questions

When we climb the stairs from the train station, a gust of wind hits Tenneh and me. It gently blows her raven locks. My backward cap stays tight on my head and seemingly covers all but a few pink strands.

No glamour today. Tenneh confirmed that Brooklynites wouldn't think twice about seeing two people who look like us walking down the street. And that was all she said about it.

The train ride here was long-drawn. When Alex and I did it in reverse, the time went by in a flash. Not once did Tenneh utter a word, nor could I see her expression behind her glasses. Matt gave her the general location of where we initially met, and I was to retrace my steps from there.

She's following the instructions from her phone being chirped by her ear device only she can hear. I'm struggling to follow someone who is not giving me any direction.

After several unexpected turns, loops, and crosswalks, I speed ahead of Tenneh and physically stand in her way.

"What is wrong, Tenneh? Why have you not spoken since we began our journey? How have I offended you?"

She takes off her glasses, and with all the charisma of a statue, she says, "We're here."

I was so focused on following Tenneh that I didn't take a moment to look at my surroundings. We're in front of the store where I met Alex. It has only been a few days, but this feels like coming back to a childhood playground. Flashes of our meeting conflate with images of Eva, and others of my sisters and I playing as children.

My turn to lead the search. I am careful not to take a misstep or make a wrong turn. Tenneh is acting like she's not in the mood to be looped around for no good reason.

We cross a few streets that look familiar and then I realize I am going in the opposite direction. The groan from my companion is audible. Even so, I try to direct her and let her know when I am turning or unsure of where to go.

After a few trials and errors, we make it to what I recognize as the park where I woke up. Except this time there is no makeshift market at the entrance.

"What's PETA?" I turn to ask Tenneh.

Taken aback by the question, she takes a few seconds before answering.

"People for the Ethical Treatment of Animals. It's an organization. Why?"

"A man in this park accused me of being a part of them."

I smile, turn around, and keep walking to the patch of grass that served as my bed.

When we get to the spot, I take a deep breath.

"If this is your connection in an unbalanced realm, I

don't want to know what you can do in yours," Tenneh quietly says. "Are you sure you want to do this? Sometimes, the mind blocks things out for our own protection."

"I need to know what happened."

I look around to make sure I ask the right beings and spot a strong large tree nearby. Once in front of it, with Tenneh covering at least one side of me, I dig my right hand deep into the ground in one fell strike and grab a root from the underground.

Tenneh sees me sweating and starting to breathe faster, as the energy from the tree pours a cacophony of feelings and memories. The ground starts to tremble at my behest.

"Breathe with me," Tenneh instructs and starts audibly inhaling and exhaling, this time in a controlled manner, careful not to conjure hurricane winds. "Close your eyes and focus on the intention. One small step leads to another."

I calm down, the ground stops trembling, and I let the energy from the tree wash over me. I can sense joyous moments of humans caring for it, the unspeakable terror of it being used to aid in the abuse of many, and the emptiness of being isolated and forgotten. The tree's energy calms itself and allows me to sense its previous interaction with mine. It was faint ... and fleeting. There was no great struggle, I learn. I happened to appear on this ground.

"This makes no sense," I mutter.

"What?"

"I appeared out of nowhere only sometime before waking up. How can that be?"

I release the root and pull my forearm from the ground.

As an appreciation, I help the tree nourish and assist its smaller neighbors to grow stronger so it won't feel so alone.

"I knew this was a waste of time," Tenneh protests, turning away from me.

"That means my last memories were not here," I say, loud enough for Tenneh to hear me. "I was not sure why I woke up here, and now I know that I was brought here. But how can I just appear out of nowhere? Can witches teleport?"

"No. Can you?"

"Not that I know of, no."

She turns around, visibly exasperated, and asks me to kneel in front of her.

"Just do it," she commands.

Once I oblige, Tenneh closes her eyes and starts muttering nondescript words, with her right thumb on my forehead and her left hand raised as if she was holding up a large object.

I am about to ask her what she is doing when my mind goes blank. I can only see white and, slowly, like a painter making brushstrokes, I see the image of the park during nighttime. No people are around, and only a golden fire in the air breaks through the darkness of the late hours. The ring of fire expands, and I see my body fall backward from it to the ground. I'm seeing into the past. Past me is gasping for air and eventually passes out. My vision goes white again, and I feel Tenneh's hand close my eyes.

When I open my eyes again, it's daytime, and Tenneh is standing over me without her glasses, looking at me and expecting answers from what we both just saw.

"You could unlock my memories this whole time and decided not to do it?"

"No. I helped you see what you already unlocked for yourself. It's not that difficult to see things from a different perspective. You just have to allow yourself to be open to the experience."

She does not take kindly to my accusation.

"We need to talk about it," she says in a softer tone.

"I am not sure I want to."

"I've never heard of a witch having the power to conjure golden fire," she says.

"My father would never do anything to harm me."

CHAPTER 23

Ambush

The train ride back to Tenneh's apartment is easier than I expected. I am still trying to make sense of what I saw and am not ready to speak it into existence yet. Tenneh is also not the best conversationalist, so it is a pretty quiet ride again, aside from a few people playing music from their bags.

Back in Tenneh's neighborhood, where we need to be careful of being spotted, she turns back to me and stares me down. No sunglasses, because there's no need for them anymore with an overcast sky.

"We can have the conversation right here and now, or we can have it in the apartment where your bounty-hunter lover can hear," she says with no discernable emotion, which in Tenneh-language I've figured out means she cares.

"There is not much to talk about."

"I beg to differ. We clearly know you were pushed, knocked unconscious, and dumped in a random park through what appeared to be conjured fire."

Those images keep coming up like vivid paintings in my mind, and every time, I'm more confused by them. And

Tenneh is throwing words out there, assessing the situation as if she knew anything about me or my family or faes.

"What do you want me to say?" I snap at her. "That you were right in this being a waste of time, and we should have focused on the portal?"

"I understand you're confused and maybe even angry, and you are right to feel that way," Tenneh says in a calming voice. "But what you're *not* going to do is snap or raise your voice at me, unless you want to be on your own."

She speaks to me as if I were the child and she were the royal. We're in the middle of a sidewalk with only but a few people walking by, and she holds her head like my mother does in court.

"So, tell me," she continues. "What was that ring of fire?"

"I am not sure," I relent. It is easier for me to answer questions than it is to formulate a thought right now. "We were taught that only the strongest of fae who perfectly embodied our tenets could produce it. It was said to defy all logic and laws, breaking reality and creating a portal."

"Love that for you guys," Tenneh rolls her eyes. "Sounds like propaganda, if you ask me."

I'm not sure what that word means, but before I can ask her, a group of three tall men comes over to us.

"Sup, beautiful," the skinnier one with the oversized black shirt says to Tenneh.

She ignores him and focuses her gaze back on me.

"Oh, so you're going to ignore me for this queer?" he says, referring to me, and the other two laugh.

"Would you prefer I focus on your queerness? Or your

rude attempt to get my attention by a display of insecurity masked in toxic masculinity?" Tenneh retorts with ease. The men remain perplexed, and in that opening, she added, "move along boys, you're not worth our time."

By the expressions of the three men, I know that Tenneh has successfully enraged them. The one in the back murmurs something that seems to agitate the one who spoke to Tenneh further.

Tenneh's almond-shaped eyes narrow to where you almost can't tell they're still open. She turns around and swings her left arm with an open palm to slap the man walking toward her.

He leans back, evades the strike, and starts laughing mockingly. "Ah, guess she's the man here, defending her lady."

The other two men take an aggressive stance toward Tenneh, and my heart starts racing. I flick my left wrist and send a strong gust that pushes them back, making one of them fall.

Tenneh laughs, and that seems to set their anger off because, once the third one gets up from the ground, they begin charging us.

Tenneh takes a moment to react, but she extends both hands and starts muttering words under her breath. I react faster and stomp my right foot forward for a wider stance and extend both arms making a fist simultaneously. The ground below their feet, all the way up to Tenneh, succumbs about a foot, making them fall down face first.

By the time they are on the ground, Tenneh finishes her incantation, and the writhing men become motionless.

If it weren't for their screams and protests, I would think Tenneh killed them.

"What did you do?" I ask incredulously.

"What did *you* do? I thought you were against harm," Tenneh retorts.

"I—they were attacking you."

"So, self-defense is valid only when you do it?"

She was referencing Alex and it angers me. But, then, it hits me.

"I was going to take Eva to meet my father," I say instinctively.

Tenneh's eyes widen, and I see her lose her composure for the first time.

"Wha—what was that leap?"

"I cannot explain it. I do not really remember it, but I can feel it," I explain. "Let us go. I need to talk to Matt."

We start hastily walking in the direction of her apartment, but something pulls me back. I jog back to the men on the ground and prop each one against the wall of a tall building on the sidewalk. They keep shouting and trying to spit on me while I do it, but I'm afraid they will get trampled or be unable to breathe for some reason.

Tenneh slowly walks back to the scene, just stares at the entire situation, and refuses to assist. "They don't deserve our kindness."

"*Our* kindness?"

"Yes, ours. I could've killed them or made this permanent. Tomorrow they'll wake up fine. I'd say that's more than they deserve."

"We are not anyone to decide who deserves what."

CHAPTER 24

Amends

Back at Tenneh's house, Matt greets us with a bright smile and the form of a stallion.

In rare form, Tenneh lets out a small scream of excitement when she sees Matt's top human half and what looks like the legs of a small horse.

"Check it out, guys," he beams. "I'm a centaur! Hooves and all."

"A satyr, at best," I joke back.

He laughs and looks down, almost embarrassed to be proud of his achievement. It's adorable and makes me feel a small needle in my heart for not being more supportive.

"That is amazing that you are able to do that in two days, Matt. Most changelings would think of you as a master," I try to overcompensate.

"I wouldn't know," he replies to no one particularly.

Tenneh and I lock eyes while Matt is busy changing his legs back to human form.

"Were they supposed to be horse legs? Hooves? Are they called something different than legs?"

Matt laughs and acknowledges, “I modeled them after horse legs, but there’s only so much mass in my body. I’d be the lightest horse in history. Anyway, how was the field trip?”

Without skipping another beat, Tenneh says, “Uneventful,” and slumps down to the floor against the wall so Grimace can climb on her lap.

The dog is not particularly thrilled by any of the developments with his new friend Matt. Just focused on the fact that his companion, Tenneh, is back and might have some treats for him.

“Some things did come up,” I admit.

Tenneh’s eyes widen, and Matt barely looks up from his own legs, trying to get them exactly right for this form.

“Do you want to go up to the roof so we may talk?”

My question catches both of them off guard, and Tenneh gets back up.

“You can have the apartment. I need to take Grimace for a walk, and I should pick up some dinner on the way,” she says.

“Let’s go to the roof anyway, Tinker Bell. I need fresh air and some hay.”

Matt smiles and walks past me, expecting me to follow. He smells like Alana and Brett, and Leslie … like Alex.

We walk up the stairs, mostly in silence.

An interesting plea to a person who can normally fly. I decide it would be best not to mention that.

Once on the roof, we notice that we’re not alone. There’s a plump older woman hand in hand with a bigger man, leaning against the veranda, watching the pink hues of a clearing sky.

Matt grabs me by the arm without me noticing and guides me back to where all the plants are. I forgot to put my cap back on, thinking we would be alone, so my hair is blowing in the wind.

I thought this would be easier, but I'm having trouble finding the words to begin this conversation.

"So, what's up?" Matt begins. "Why do you hate me now?"

He asks the question with a smile, yet the smile doesn't quite meet his eyes. I immediately feel contrite.

"I do not hate you," I begin. "We met under the strangest of circumstances, and I unfairly placed the pressure of my life on you. A great deal of what I feel toward you is guilt."

"Eh. I knew what you asked of me, and I decided to help."

"I guess. But that dinner with Brett—"

"Yeah, yeah, that dinner. Whatever, man. Like, I thought that even though we spent only a small amount of time together, you wouldn't be so judge-y about my past. Especially given the welcoming I got from you after I spent a few days away. Or was that only because Brett is hot?"

There are so many things he's saying that I want to correct. Yet one thing is true, and I owe it to him to explain myself.

"The tenets that fae—"

"Don't give me that crap," he interrupts me again. "You

don't really abide by them, and even if you did, you know that life is not that black and white. Give me a break."

Matt is getting visibly upset. All this animosity is bubbling under the surface. He is one smile away from shouting. One wink away from a glare.

"There is a line, Alex! There is a clear line between right and wrong. And you can take fae tenets out of the equation, but at the end of the day you acted as an executioner of a being."

"Of a being that was about to kill my mother!" he replies.

Tears pile up in his eyes. Even though we aren't shouting, our voices must have carried, because the plump woman is walking over to us.

"Excuse me," she says with a demanding tone. "This is not a place for a lovers' quarrels. Some of us are trying to enjoy the view."

"Get the hell out of my face," Matt responds. "And mind your business."

I know he means those words toward me as he voices them. At least, that's how I take them. But the woman isn't as understanding of Matt's tone or exhortation. With a gaping mouth and frowned brow, she storms off back to the veranda where we can hear her recounting the tale of seconds ago to the man she is with.

"We could have handled that better," I tell Matt, shouldering some of the blame that was meant to fall solely on his back. "And I understand self-defense. All I am saying is that we always have a choice, and it is our actions that define who we are."

"So, I'm nothing but a murderer to you? Is that why you've been so hot and cold with me?"

It feels like the conversation is going nowhere, and I'm running out of time before Matt leaves me for good this time. He wipes away a few tears that broke the dam and holds the further flow of waterworks by pursing his lips.

"It is not like—"

"Excuse me, gentlemen," the large man is next to us now.

It's as if I must be sure of every sentence and be ready to blurt it, or someone will interrupt me.

"I think you owe my girl an apology," the man says, looking at Matt.

I see Matt start to turn red and begin inflating his size. Before he can speak, I try to take this burden from him.

"No, he does not," I say. "We are having a conversation on a roof at a normal volume, and you two are being very rude right now. Please, walk back to your partner, and like my friend said, mind your business."

The man chuckles and crosses his arms. "Or what?"

"Oh, please," I roll my eyes and smirk, mostly to show Matt support in this inane argument. Before he or Matt can say or do anything, I make a fist with my right hand, lift it in front of the man's face, and quickly show him my palm. A flash of blinding light hits him, and I flick my left wrist as a controlled gust pushes him back to the veranda, but not strong enough to make him lose his balance.

Confused as to what is happening, the couple rushes to the door to go back down, but not before the woman gives me one last glare.

With the couple gone, Matt and I have the roof to

ourselves. I turn to him and muster a small smile, almost seeking approval or recognition for handling the situation.

"Not only are you a hypocrite, but you also just displayed your weird magic to strangers in a heavily monitored area."

That comment takes me aback. I thought I was doing a good thing, something he would be proud of me for doing. And it was rewarded with snark and scolding.

I feel my face getting warm, and I fight back tears. Matt sees me, and his demeanor changes in an instant. His shoulders slump and, if I didn't know any better, he lowers in stature.

"Um, I mean, c'mon," he stumbles and fiddles with his hair. "That was nice of you, but you're putting us at risk here."

At this moment, I can't imagine why I would be mad at this person. How can someone who is so caring could simultaneously be capable of such a reprehensible act? I remember how I felt when I thought they left me and how inexplicably happy I was when they came back. I realize that we're arguing right now, but that wasn't my intention. And seeing them pause the sparring to check on their opponent tells me everything I wish I could convey to them.

I take a step closer to Matt and wipe the few tears on my face. His face changes from compassion to confusion. I smirk because he makes the same expression in all his forms when they're confused. I place my left hand at the back of his neck and pull his face to meet mine. I kiss his static lips, and, for a moment, I'm mortified that he does not reciprocate. Every second is an eternity. I pull away, afraid that I'm doing something terribly wrong. Once I do, I can see the shock on Matt's face.

"I am so sorry," I say, probably two decibels short of a shout.

"Listen, I—," he begins with pain in his eyes.

"No, no. It is fine. I apologize for doing that. There is a lot of emotion, and every form you take is attractive. I am really, really, sorry. I will be on my way."

"Elior, stop," Matt says with finality.

My body just freezes in place. My mind is so scattered that my body welcomes any given direction as to what to do with itself.

"That's not how you resolve issues," he continues. "You can't just wash away what you think of me with what you feel for me. It doesn't work like that. I've been wanting to kiss you since our first conversation but not like this."

I should've left when I had the chance. I'd rather wake up confused and without any memory again than to feel his rejection.

"Level with me here," Matt says in a soft voice. "What do you really think of me?"

Can I make it to the door in time? This would be a good time for my wings to be working.

"I think you are an amazing, kind, funny, and smart being. I also think you are capable of heinous acts. I think you compensate for those acts by striving to make those around you feel good. And I am trying to reconcile that those things can exist within the same person."

"That's fair."

"I did not kiss you to end the dialogue," I explain. Still,

I can't bring myself to look at him directly, so I avert my gaze between the ground and the potted plants behind him. "I did it because, with one single act, you showed me what I was trying to tell you. That you are able to not like someone in the moment, but that does not diminish your affection for them. That is not a common quality, which I think makes you special. And I wanted a taste of that."

Matt just stands there in silence. Time begins to crawl again. He walks in my direction, and, as he passes me, he smiles and says, "Give me an equally strong reason for me to want a taste."

He opens the door and walks down the stairs, leaving me with the dark sky, the wind, and the plants.

It's a nice sentiment from Matt. It leaves me hopeful and feeling a little less rejected than before, but ultimately it's the same as parallel lines promising to meet. Tomorrow night during the full moon, I hope to find the portal and make it back home safely. Matt, Leslie, Farrah, Brett, Alana, and Alex will remain in this realm, where they will be safe.

CHAPTER 25

Asylum

At dinner with Matt and Tenneh that night, you would never have known that moments before he and I had an emotional conversation. He is all smiles and jokes, and to my surprise, Tenneh is joking alongside him.

They had a rocky start, but Matt and Tenneh seem to bounce off each other as if they've known each other for some time. Every so often in conversation, Matt will change his appearance to reference what they call "celebs," to the amusement of Tenneh. I am just … there.

Jealousy creeps in. I feel some sort of ownership over Matt. And he wouldn't have met Tenneh if he weren't trying to help *me* in the first place. Yet, I'm the foreign one in this conversation being excluded from the jokes and relegated to the background. I just want to be alone. But I know that if I leave the table, it will be taken as a slight at them, which I desperately want to do.

Eventually, Matt changes to Farrah for some reason and goes to sleep, leaving me on the couch with a reluctant Grimace.

By morning, I wake before Farrah and Tenneh, and I start walking around the apartment. So many days trapped here, and I had not thought to look around more closely. I haven't been fair to Tenneh and tried to get to know her as Alex has. I figure there must be something around here that could give me a hint as to what I can do to show her my appreciation for her help, albeit self-interested.

There's a ladder-like ensemble that Tenneh uses as a bookcase. Some of them are colorful collections filled with drawings and thought bubbles; others look almost archaic. Tenneh handed me some to keep me occupied while she attended to clients. Some I've read already, although I couldn't understand much. And one I think I recognize: *The Great War*.

My heart starts racing. It can't be.

It can't be that we've been looking for something that was a few steps away all this time.

"Tenneh!" I scream, furious.

I don't have to turn around to know they're both wide awake after booming my voice. My nostrils are flaring, keeping pace with my heavy breathing.

There's some rumbling coming from Farrah. But this isn't about her right now.

Tenneh gets out of bed. As she walks over to me, she adjusts her robe.

"I know you are *not* screaming in my house," she says sternly. "You better explain yours—"

"What is this?" I ask while holding up the tome without turning around to face her, with my hand shaking.

She takes a moment to answer and returns to her emotionless tone and even-keel volume.

"I have no idea. It was in my aunt's collection. It seemed rare, so I kept it."

My hand grips the book so intensely that I'm afraid it'll crumble in my palm.

"You are lying, witch."

"Elior, what the hell is wrong with you?" Farrah jumps in.

I turn around to face them both. My jaw is clenched, and my eyes dart to Tenneh's half-closed ones.

"You had this all this time and did not think to mention you had all the leads here?"

"Since you clearly know more than I do about what secrets I keep, why don't you enlighten us?" Tenneh mocks. "I'm sure Farrah and Grimace would love to also know why you're one more accusation away from being slapped around and thrown out of my home."

"I would love to see you try," I respond. My left fist is now engulfed in a flame.

"You're so annoying," Farrah protests. "Why are you so angry? What is that book?"

"This is the answer we have been trying to piece together," I shake the book toward Farrah. "*The Great War* is how most nonhumans find the fae realm."

Tenneh furrows her brow, and Farrah's jaw drops.

"You're able to read it?" Tenneh asks.

"Read—no." Why would that even be a question? "Your people wrote it after mine had to leave this realm. It is revisionist history at best."

"Why don't you try reading it, then? Find your portal," Tenneh says without an ounce of emotion.

She proved me right. I knew trusting a dark magic wielder was a bad idea.

I look down at the book and see the title clearly, *The Great War,* written in golden cursive letters. There is no author. The flame on my fist extinguishes, and I start flipping through the pages in hopes of spotting a map or a chapter signaling the portals to Lempara.

The more I turn the pages, the more I can't understand the words on them. I turn the same page back and forth, and the words scramble themselves more and more with every turn.

"What the ..."

"Exactly," Tenneh says and walks over to the kitchen.

"Can you not fix this?" I ask in a lower tone, still demanding.

"It's a lock, and I don't have the key."

Tenneh heads to the kitchen and fills her kettle with water, but instead of placing it over the small flamethrower table, like she usually does, she holds it with her right hand over the open flame she manifested on her left hand. Throughout the entire process, she does not break eye contact with me.

I place the book down on the table in front of the couch. I slump on the couch, and my anger manages to manifest itself as tears.

Farrah picks up the book.

"You cry too much," Tenneh says from the kitchen with no judgment, just noting a fact.

"What good is dark magic?" I shout to no one in particular. "I was always told to fear it. That it could do things that our energy shifting could not. I have seen you, Tenneh, conjure flames as I do. And I have seen you mutter spells in another language that renders people limp. But jumbled words are the limit of your skills?"

"That's uncalled for," Farrah says to Tenneh, sitting down on the chair facing the couch I'm sitting on with the book in hand. "That being said, we don't really know what you *can* do. So, while uncalled for, the question *is* valid."

Farrah is trying to soften the blow of my comment. I appreciate the gesture. I'm not sure if I should be angry at Tenneh right now, or at Farrah for jumping in, or myself, or the book. I just know my veins are pumping steam, and it needs to be let out.

"You don't need to know what I can or cannot do," Tenneh simply says with tea in hand. "Why didn't you say there was a book with directions on where to find your house?"

"It is not … it is not a detailed map. From what I was told, nonhumans in this realm used it to cross-reference passed down knowledge and find our portals. The few copies that were made were destroyed at Lempara once refugees crossed."

"Interesting," says Tenneh, now looking at her phone. "You sell it as a sanctuary from this realm but leave no way for those looking for it to find it."

Such an insipid answer. She's not letting it show, but she's upset I yelled at her and now needs to have the moral high ground on issues she knows nothing about.

"Nice try. The fae have done expeditions to find communities and offer them to come."

"With closed portals?"

She does not look up.

"That is your people's fault," I say. "Regardless, there are few nonhumans left in this realm."

"I'm here," Farrah says.

Tenneh and I lock eyes. There's a moment of silence among the three of us. Only Grimace's heavy breathing can be heard.

"Yes. Yes, you are," I break the silence, trying to come up with the words as they fall out of my mouth. "But you are so close to humans, and it is not like changelings were ever in any danger. If someone found out what they were, they would just change forms. I heard some even killed the humans who discovered them and then lived their victim's lives."

I couldn't shut myself up. My brain just looked up changelings and started spouting any information I knew about them.

Farrah doesn't seem fazed, though.

"With your wings retracted, you pass for human," she retorts. "What's the difference?"

I see Tenneh draw a small smile in between sips of tea.

"I ... I do not know," I relent.

Here's my chance to share with Farrah what happened to her kind. It somehow doesn't feel appropriate to shift the conversation so drastically and let this potential lead go to waste on the night of a full moon.

I let out a heavy sigh. I feel ashamed that I overreacted

with Tenneh, although I still feel justified. She could have brought it up at any moment, and used every tool at her disposal to find the portal. Maybe more time with her just means more time to harvest our blood. Perhaps this was all a mistake, and I should've stayed put in that park and waited until my father came back for me.

"*Elusive as they are, horned horses, also called unicorns, can be drawn to out of their habitats by providing a serene altar with plenty of fruit …*" huh.

Tenneh immediately gets up from her seat, and I look up at Farrah.

"What?" she says, darting her eyes between mine and Tenneh's. "It's kind of hard to read, but you can still do it if you stare at it long enough."

"Are you joking right now?" Tenneh asks with seriousness on her face.

Looking slighted by Tenneh's comment, Farrah opens to the first page of the book and stares at the page for a few seconds before starting to read aloud.

"Those who seek shall find their way," she says.

Tenneh rushes to hover over Farrah. She stares at the page in the same manner Farrah did a few seconds ago but only looks frustrated.

"The stupid key is intention," Tenneh says to herself, loud enough for the room to hear.

"Let me try again," I say excitedly, extending my hand to Farrah, almost grabbing the book from her if I could reach.

Farrah hands me the book, and I close my eyes and concentrate on finding my way back home. I picture Lempara, my family, and my seat at court. I open my eyes once more and … nothing. The words make no sense to me.

"That can't be it," I tell Tenneh as I get up to hand the book back to Farrah and stand next to Tenneh. "Who is seeking something more than I am."

"Clearly, her."

We both look down at Farrah, who doesn't seem too thrilled about the kind of attention she's getting this morning.

In order to take some pressure from Farrah, I volunteer myself to get breakfast for everyone. Tenneh informs me that it is too early for vendors to be available, but she does have something for her and me to do together so we can leave Farrah to read.

After having a tea myself, I join Tenneh by the table, where she keeps the small vials with unidentifiable items and herbs in.

"That's bay leaf, Elior. You cook with it," she says and rolls her eyes when I stare too long at a small vial with dead leaves.

I look over at Farrah and fight the urge to ask her to go through the pages in order when I see her just going to random pages back and forth.

She *is* taking notes, thankfully.

"Very well, what are we doing?"

Tenneh turns to me with some empty vials in hand.

"You're brewing your own glamour for today."

My heart lurches the bottom of my stomach. It's one thing to passively be involved in dark magic. It's a completely different situation when you have to do it yourself.

"I do not know if I am comfortable with that, Tenneh."

"You don't have to be comfortable with everything you do. Sometimes, you just do it because it's the right thing to do, your highness."

She pushes the vials to my chest, so I'm forced to hold them.

Tenneh turns to the icebox and pulls one vial I immediately recognize. Alex's blood.

"You wanted to know what my magic can do, right? Here's your chance to get your hands dirty."

"Why are you using Farrah's blood?"

"Because I found a way to combine it with the glamour brew. So not only can we distinguish each other, we can mimic her ability to onlookers, if only briefly."

"Tenneh, listen, I just—"

She keeps shoving ingredients from the icebox at me while reciting instructions on what to do with them.

"First, you lay out all the ingredients. And you thank them for life and their use after it."

I'm facing a table with plants, animal limbs, and entrails. It's taking everything in me not to throw up at the sight of such a massacre. All I want to do is apologize to these beings, not thank them.

My protesting eyes are swatted by a commanding stare.

"Now, water is the source of life. So, go ahead and fill that pot there halfway, and we can bring some life to our new friends."

I do as she commands.

"First, throw in the leaves with the appreciation of their quiet growth. Add enough that you can't see the bottom of the pot. Then, you add the frog entrails with the acknowledgment of change and metamorphosis. Now, we wait until it's boiling."

It doesn't take long for the water to boil. I want this whole experience to be done quickly, so I make the fire under the pot hotter myself.

"Good. Now, add the octopus tentacles with the intention of concealment. And please make sure you are connecting with each ingredient, Elior. Let it boil for a few minutes."

While we wait for the cadavers to boil, I glance over at Farrah, who is distracted by Grimace. I apparently inhale and exhale so loudly, it attracts her and Grimace's attention. Farrah promptly gets back to the book.

"You can strain the water into this container," Tenneh instructs. "Then, in the smaller pot, you're going to throw in some fresh water with two tablespoons of honey, those mint leaves, and lemon peels."

"Am I supposed to have an intention with these ingredients?" I ask nervously, half expecting this to be the part where she invokes death.

"Sweetness? I don't know, that's just for flavoring," she responds without too much thought.

While I'm tending to the smaller pot, Tenneh goes to the strained water in the container with the vial of Alex's blood. She takes a dropper and mixes in three drops of blood into the water while reciting in Latin, "Et non opus est tibi ut gloriam."

"Now," she continues, "strain that and pour it into those small jars only halfway."

We can't possibly be done already.

Tenneh takes a ladle and goes after me, filling the small jars with the tainted water to the brim.

She places them all together and hovers both hands above them and starts chanting a series of words over and over.

"Peccatum meum sanctificetur gloriam meam et feci."

"That's it," Tenneh declares.

I'm baffled by the simplicity of the process and the amount of intention and honor of life that it involves.

"Why doesn't every human just do this?"

"You kind of have to be born with the gift," she says and, in rare form, wiggles her fingers making them glitter.

She takes the vials and places them on the table by the door.

"Please wash the pots, Elior. Thanks."

If I did not know any better, I would have taken great offense to this request a few days ago. But I know that she does not have help to do it for her, which is her way of punishing me for the earlier shouting.

Seeing that Tenneh is done with her brew, Farrah pokes her nose away from the book and says, to no one in particular, that she's finding out about my kind.

"I would not take those details seriously, Farrah," I explain. "Humans wrote it from their perspective, so I doubt there is much validity to their interpretations of fae culture."

"Says here your wings act as their own beings with knowledge of fae's past," Farrah says as a statement of fact, which I can't remember right now whether it's true or not.

How could I forget something so intrinsically mine?

"Whatever happened to you," Farrah says, looking at me now with compassion in her eyes, "someone didn't want you to go back to your realm."

My chest tightens. It all comes crashing down on me at once. Whether this book is right or not is not the issue. It's the fact that I can't tell whether it's true or not.

Farrah's right. Something, or someone, doesn't want me back in Lempara.

"Eva did not do this," I say to myself.

"What?" Tenneh asks.

"She wants to find the portal, too. She does not know that I do not remember how to find it."

"Does that change anything?" Tenneh continues to probe.

"Depends on what Farrah finds in that book."

Tenneh seems confused. After a few moments, she flips her braids back and, with both hands on her hips, says, "You need to go to Central Park now. Maybe being close to a more natural environment will guide your reading. Your surroundings impact you more than you think. I'm sure it's the same for that book."

"Elior," Tenneh says firmly. "Take all the vials with you, so they last you until the night."

"Are you not coming with us?" Farrah asks.

"I have to get some materials, but I don't want to hold you guys up. I'll meet you at the park before sundown."

It finally feels like gears are moving, and there's a chance that tonight I'll be back in Lempara. It also feels like a small needle piercing my heart at the thought of saying goodbye to Alex.

CHAPTER 26

Awkward

Knowing what the vials contain now makes me squeamish to drink them. Pleasant notes of honey and citrus aside, I just ingested the brew of corpses and the blood of my friend.

Farrah wanted to change into a Brett-like form, but ultimately decided it would attract more attention than it could afford us advantages. The walk and train ride with Leslie are mostly quiet. I am relieved that Leslie is nose-deep into *The Great War.* I feel too awkward about our last conversation to muster another one-on-one interaction.

Once in a while, Leslie comes up to share tidbits of what she is reading.

"Did you know humans tried to broker a peace treaty with nonhumans?"

Lie.

"Did you know that you can only fly up to a certain height in this realm?"

Unsure.

"Did you know the fae accords proposed portals be established in every major world city, as humanity grew?"

True.

She wasn't really looking for a response. It was nice to hear her muse over new knowledge and see her face light up with what she thought were interesting facts.

Leslie calls a bluff on the existence of sphinxes, and, when I assure her they did actually exist at one point, her jaw almost hits the floor. Yet another thing humans wiped out.

I'm thankful the book is giving us something else to focus on rather than ourselves.

"You know," Leslie says. "I'm learning more about you in this book than from what you've told me yourself."

All inaccuracies, probably.

"People usually know who I am, so I guess I have never had to practice."

"I'm not talking about your title or position, Tinker Bell," Leslie says, and it makes my heart beat fast to hear her call me a name again. "I'm talking about who you are as a person. It says here the fae live by certain tenets, which you won't shut up about, but it also says that some fae didn't agree with the accords and sided with the humans. So even fae have free will, it seems."

She says it as a way to engage in conversation about who I am, but it irks me that humans would lie like that I realize.

"Maybe I do not know who I am yet," I say facetiously.

It's a throwaway comment that, unfortunately, gains meaning when verbalized.

The expression on my face must change because Leslie's eyes go from attentive to pitying.

"You don't have to know who you are at any given moment. We're constantly changing, growing, and building upon the previous iterations of ourselves," Leslie says. "I think what's important is knowing for yourself what is right and wrong in this life, then just striving to be a little bit better every time."

We get to our stop, and Leslie packs the book in a shoulder bag Tenneh lent her. I let her lead the way.

CHAPTER 27

Volleyball

Finally, we arrive at Central Park. I like this place.

The cool breeze is blowing strongly enough to move my shirt and graze my wings.

Humans seem happier here—more at ease with each other. Some are even playing netter ball.

Leslie stops at a cart and asks the man for some bottled waters before we arrive at a large fountain in front of a small lake.

It's simultaneously jarring and pleasant to see nature with human intervention—a respite in a desolate yet crowded city.

We walk for a while before settling by some rocks in the periphery of a marked field. It feels good to sit on the ground. I take a cue from the people around me and remove my shoes, while Leslie reclines against a large boulder with *The Great War*.

I'm feeling impatient for her to find something of use, but I'm trying not to place any more pressure on Leslie. Besides, had we not found the book, the plan was always to come here and talk to the entire park under the full moon to find the portal. The blaring sun prompts me to move to lay on top of the rock that Leslie is leaning against.

Even with my eyes closed while lying down, I sense something coming toward us. I'm only fast enough to open my eyes and see a white ball the size of a human head coming directly at Leslie. I lift my right arm as quickly as my reflexes allow me, but the gust of wind I summon only lifts the ball high enough to hit me on my right side.

"Whoa, I'm sorry, man."

The low husky voice is coming from a tanned shirtless man with long brown hair tied in a knot. If it's not for the fact that he is shirtless and I can't see wings, I could swear he was fae.

"Pass it back?" he asks, referring to the ball that now sits by Leslie's feet.

I just stare and say nothing.

Leslie kicks back the ball without paying too much attention to the interaction. He picks up the ball and, along with it, the chances of asking him who he is.

"Are you playing netter ball?" I blurt out, immediately regretting the choice.

"What-ball?" he turns around to ask with a smile.

"What are you playing?" I say as I dismount the boulder. Something inside me is pulling me toward this man.

Leslie has a skeptical look on her face, so I just focus on the man standing in front of us.

"We're playing volleyball if you guys wanna join," the man says, pointing to two people nearby.

"Thanks. Studying," Leslie responds before I can formulate a coherent thought.

"No probs," replies the fae-looking man.

It is still late morning on the most important mission of my life, but I need to know this person who so easily has captured my focus. It's an instinctual pull that I can't pin down. Besides, I could use a break from the awkward silences between Leslie and myself.

"May I join?" I yell loud enough for the man to hear me. The portal, Leslie, Tenneh. It all goes to the back of my mind and I want to find out who this man is.

He turns around to wave me over.

I turn to Leslie, "Do you mind?"

She waves me off.

I run over to the glistening man and his friends.

"Hello, I am Elior," I say, half-expecting my name to resonate with him or any of his friends. When it doesn't, I'm only thinking of Alex and how upset she was when I so casually revealed my name to a stranger.

"Nice to meet you, Elior. I'm Rahim. And this is Farha and Priya," he points to the two girls in the group.

"We can do teams now!" Farha says. "How good are you, Elior?"

Still unsure of the human rules for this game, I can't really assess.

"Not great?" I say.

"You're with Rahim then," Priya laughs. "Skins versus shirts!"

It takes me a moment to understand what she means by that. Panic jolts from my head all the way down to my bare feet. Will the new glamour account for additional appendages?

If I hesitate any longer, it will seem like I'm hiding something. So I just take off my shirt and hope they don't scream or bring too much attention to my wings.

"Sick tats, man," Rahim says.

A small part of me is disappointed that Rahim didn't recognize them as wings. I was kind of hoping that he is fae. Then I realize that the glamour is probably making my wings seem like body markings.

I look over to Leslie, who now seems to be directing her sight to us more often.

I am half annoyed that she is not reading further, and half excited that I can draw her attention away.

"I'll start," Rahim says, as he holds the ball with his left hand and punches it in the air from below with his right.

Priya volleys it, passing the ball to her partner. Farha gives a little jump and slams the ball with her left hand toward Rahim and me.

My instincts kick in, and before Rahim reacts, I lunge forward and counter with both my hands.

This is the same as netter ball.

Unsure whether it's the thrill of playing a game or feeling the sun on my wings, but I am feeling recharged.

After a few hits back and forth, keeping the ball in the air, Rahim gives me a small nod, thinking I know what he means by this signal.

When the ball comes back again to our side, I volley it over to him, and he slams it with all his force over to the girls. Farha throws herself over, hits the ball again, and shifts the momentum to send it flying upward. The ball is coming down far behind Rahim and me with full force. I run back and jump, with some assistance from manipulated air. I'm able to hit the ball, and it lands squarely between Farha and Priya.

On my way back to the group, my three new friends are applauding and cheering me on, and Leslie is walking to join the group.

"That was incredible, Elior!" Farha cheers.

"I've never seen moves like that," Rahim chimes in.

"Right? I don't think just any *person* can do that?" Leslie says, joining the group.

"Oh, it was nothing, really," I laugh nervously.

Leslie's face turns to a scowl when Rahim stares at me with a smile.

"We better get going, Tink—Elior," Leslie says. "Tenneh is meeting up with us soon."

"Aw man, that sucks that we only had you for one match," Rahim interjects.

"You're welcome to play with us any time," Priya says as she lets her silky raven hair out from the binds of a hair tie.

There's a certain tension to this interaction that I cannot particularly explain.

Rahim comes closer to me. I'm still inspecting his brown skin, glistening with sweat, for any markings of contracted wings.

"I'd love to meet up and play together again," he says softly. "Can I get your number?"

"He doesn't have one," Leslie answers before my vocal

cords are able to even rumble. “And he’s moving out of town today, so there’s lots on the agenda.”

“Oh no, that’s a shame. Where are you moving to?” Farha asks.

“Um … back home to …”

I’m blanking on human realm places.

“Ontario. He’s Canadian,” Leslie saves me. She’s clearly impatient with this conversation.

“I guess I’ll just hope for fate to bring us together again,” Rahim leans in for a hug.

He throws his arms around me, and I feel electricity run through my body. He keeps holding tight for far too long. Meanwhile, I can see Farha and Priya approach Leslie.

Noticing something’s wrong, Leslie extends her arm and pushes them back.

“Don’t bother with her!” Rahim yells. “We got the prince.”

CHAPTER 28

Brawl

The fog is as quick as it is thick. Rahim's weather manipulation manages to make a public park seem intimate.

Farha and Priya don't listen to Rahim's instruction and lunge toward Leslie. Rahim has managed to rope me with some thick plastic cord from his wristbands, strapping my arms to my sides.

I'm trying to get a clear shot of Farha and Priya to blow some wind in order to separate them from Leslie, but I notice Rahim pull a small black stick from his pocket. I recognize it as a smaller version of Shoto's lightning stick. I shift my weight to my left leg and, with my right leg, kick a strong gust that sends Rahim flying back.

"I am sorry," I say involuntarily.

I start running like a penguin on ice toward Leslie, who I see has knocked out Farha. But Priya is hurling fireballs of her creation at her.

Leslie is successfully dodging and retaliating by throwing rocks from the ground. At a seeming standstill, Priya aims a fireball at Leslie's bag.

Afraid she would destroy my only strong ticket home, I flick both wrists to the left, hurling the fireball back to its creator. It hits Priya, on the shin, but before I can see how she counters, I'm hit by a wet whip.

Rahim.

He runs back to me with two fists the size of pumpkins with how much water he has around them.

They seem like fae warriors.

"Thanks for making it fun, your highness," he yells as he runs in a direct path.

I thought my father's commanders taught their warriors to do better than that. Or maybe he's underestimating a bound prince.

His mistake. I'm ready to endure some pain today.

I hop with both legs in the air and land them to make the ground in his path crack up to him. He, in turn, stops in his tracks and jumps in the air so as to not lose his balance and continues running along the lifted rocky road. I turn my head down to my right arm and blow fire at myself.

I can either scream in pain or keep blowing until the binding breaks. Then, I think of Leslie.

I choose the latter.

The strange rope finally breaks in time for me to flow Rahim's water whip to the side. My right arm is now badly burned. It hurts to lift it, so I keep countering Rahim's water whips one-handed. He's unrelenting and successfully pushing me back.

"Why are you doing this?" I shout at him, not really expecting an answer.

"It's either you or me, your highness," he says with a grin.

He speaks as a fae that was left no choice but revels in the pursuit of violence. Our soldiers are meant to restrain and resolve conflict, not instigate it.

"You are no subject of mine or Lempara," I respond. Lifting my left knee to my chest and stomping it on the ground, I cause a tree trunk-sized ground brick to hit him squarely in the chest, knocking him out. Two puddles of water fall to his sides.

The fog begins to subside with Rahim knocked out.

I turn my attention over to Leslie, who I can see is now face down on the ground with her feet and hands tied behind her back.

"No!" I scream at the sight of Leslie helplessly watching as Priya burns *The Great War*.

She turns to me and quickly glances at Rahim on the ground. With no visible markings, bright, glittering, translucent fae wings extend from her back, and she takes flight.

Priya is hurling fireballs from the sky so fast that it's impossible to dodge them all as she chases behind me.

I'm tempted to go back and check Rahim and Farha for wings, but the projectile fireballs dissuade me from it.

I take a page from Alex's book and jump flip backward, letting Priya fly slightly ahead of me. Once I land and she notices what I did, I inhale deeply and lift both arms high in the sky and slam them hard against the ground I am standing on.

With no wind beneath her, her wings are useless, and Priya falls to the ground. She does land beautifully, though.

"Give it up, your highness," Priya says, and I could swear it sounds like a plea more than a command.

She continues hurling fireballs at me, walking on a straight line with no level of haste.

"You do not have to do this, Priya. Please," I say, as I keep swatting her projectiles with ease, which become fewer and fewer as she approaches.

She stops only a few feet away, and I can see tears coming down her face. At that moment, I realize she was never aiming to hit Leslie or myself. She was only trying to corral us.

"Priya, are you all right? How can I help you?"

Between tears, she says loud enough for me to hear her unequivocally, "Is Rahim dead?"

My body tenses up, and I feel the chill in the air.

"I … I do not know," I say. "I was not intending for that. I just wanted him to stop attacking me. Is Farha alive?"

Knowing what Leslie is capable of, I am not sure I want to hear the answer to that question. But Priya just nods.

"Just come with us, and it will all be over," Priya adds.

"Did my father send you?" I realize it's unorthodox, but if this is the king's way to show displeasure while rescuing me, I'll take it.

Priya's eyes widen, her brow furrows, and mouth falls slightly agape. She looks offended at the mere mention of my father.

"You and he are going to be the end of us. Eva was—"

Like an underground train arriving at the platform, Priya is hit on the side by two massive black hairy arms, unable to finish her thought.

I'm horrified at the sight of what I think is Leslie. A bizarre amalgamation of parts all amounting to her is standing before me.

Leslie remained herself, for the most part, changing her legs to that of a horse—or maybe a goat? And what I can only imagine are ape or maybe gorilla arms?

"What did you do?" I scream at Leslie, as I rush to check on Priya.

"Are you joking? These hood rats were trying to kill us!" Leslie yells back. "And thanks for helping me. Really nice touch there."

"You do not get it," I fight back. "She is fae. They are all fae. This was a trap, yes, but they would never actually kill us."

Priya's wings have lost some of their glimmer. My heart starts beating faster, and it makes me hyper-aware of the amount of space it occupies in my chest. I check her wrist. No pulse. Her neck. No pulse.

Mine is racing.

I place my head on her chest to listen for a heartbeat.

It's there. Faint, but there.

I exhale in relief.

"I get that they're fae. That doesn't change the fact that they attacked us, Elior. A wrong hit or a misfire, and I could have died."

Leslie is justifying her actions and she is technically correct. But right now, my thoughts are being pulled in a million directions.

The fog is now completely gone, and my wings let me know the sun is shining back on them.

"You do not think I was trying to help you? I think I killed my own kind for you!" I scream from the ground at the top of my lungs.

Rahim.

My mind reminds me to check in on Leslie, assuage her concerns, and soothe her doubts. But my body gets up and runs over to check on Rahim.

There's a faint heartbeat. Bless Lempara.

As I run back to Leslie, I know I am doing everything wrong with her. I hope I still have some goodwill with her to understand that these are my people—beings I was sworn to protect.

"Leslie, I am so sorry for raising my voice earlier. How are you doing?"

She rolls her eyes at me and changes back to her normal human Leslie form, sans gorilla arms, and horse legs.

"We need to leave. Now."

Leslie pulls me by the hand. We're hastily walking past park goers horrified at the sight of the destroyed landscape and three people on the ground.

"We need to change," Leslie instructs once we get between some bushes. "I honestly don't know how people are going to justify thick fog in the middle of a summer afternoon."

Teeth clenched and fists balled, I squeeze every part of my body, hoping it will do the trick in changing my appearance.

"You look constipated, Tinker Bell. What, pray tell, are you doing?"

As I open my eyes and look up, Alex has the appearance

of Rahim? Some details are different but close. Hair was lighter and longer, and he was sporting forest green eyes. Definitely resembling fae.

"I am trying to change forms," I explain. "Did it work?"

He looks at me, almost holding back a laugh that lets me know I did something wrong. I could have a third ear on my forehead for all I know.

"You look exactly the same. But you have your long hair back."

Disappointment over my lack of drastic change is assuaged by the fact that I have my hair back. I look like myself again. What better way to return to Lempara?

My mind quickly reminds me that the effects of the "Alex glamour" will wear off eventually, which means I will go back to my short-haired form.

"Why are you looking like that? What am I to call you now, Alex?"

"Rohin?" Alex muses. "And, to answer your unnecessary question, because someone is clearly looking for you in covert. I figured that if we sort of look like the Terrible Three back there, we won't attract as much attention as you'd think. Sort of like hiding in plain sight, kind of thing. Tenneh was right to make the 'glamour max.'"

I quickly decide to keep to myself that they probably found me because I blabbed about my name.

"How do I change my appearance to match yours?"

"Try to match Priya's. She was cute, albeit fiery and murderous," Rohin says. "You have to visualize in your mind exactly what you want—every detail. From the way your hair falls to the size of your toes. Then, try to feel every part of your body as if it were a limb and contort it to fit that image."

I close my eyes and try to concentrate on the image of a slightly modified Priya.

"To be honest," Rohin interrupts, "visualizing just might do it. It's a glamour; you're not actually morphing your body."

Once again, I breathe in, clear my mind, and breathe out. I keep visualizing Priya and borrow some features from my own sisters. After a few breaths, I open my eyes and find Rohin just staring back at me with boredom in his eyes.

"Did it work now?"

"Sure did. You look like a lavender-haired Bollywood star."

"Again, I don't really know what—"

Rohin holds one finger up in the air and fishes his phone out of his pocket. After reading something and replying, he says, "Let's meet up with Tenneh."

My stomach and my mind churn together in a reminder that her aunt's book is now destroyed.

"Did you tell her?" I ask, afraid of the response.

"About the book? Not yet. But whatever. She couldn't read it anyway," he says and starts walking. "Besides, I think I got what we needed from it."

Rohin turns back and smirks.

I trail behind him, looking back at the people starting to gather around Farha, Priya, and Rahim. I can still hear the commotion, but I have to fight the urge to go help and continue walking toward my ticket home.

CHAPTER 29

Portal

In a woodland area, covered by winding paths, flourishing flora, and distracted humans, we can finally sit down and pretend we're having a long conversation.

During any other circumstances, this would be an ideal place to have some one-on-one time with Alex, but alas, the threat of disarray in an entire realm shuns away romance from infiltrating our conversation.

The wooden bench we're sitting on is hard and uncomfortable. It is the only thing I can fixate my mind on without yelling at Rohin to hurry up and talk.

"I do not like this bench," I simply say.

"You want to go to another one?"

More walking. Less talking.

"No. This will do. Can I ask what important information you found out from the book now?"

Rohin smiles, leans back, and turns to me with his right arm on the backrest.

"We were right about the wings," he says. "They do have their own muscle memory and instincts. That means we were also right about someone blocking you from your own knowledge. But your wings answer to your own spirit. Just as you can feel connected to nature and shift its energy to your will, your wings have to be connected to your spirit."

I'm pretty sure that at another time, this talk would have made more sense, and it would only require a few moments of meditation. Right now, it feels as if Rohin is speaking another language. I do not know where to even begin when it comes to my spirit. And this is all from a human's perspective. It could send us on a wild goose chase that leads nowhere.

"Did it say anything about how to connect with my spirit?"

"I was getting to that before you decided to play volleyball with Team Rocket," he tilts his head, eyes squinting at me. "Not to worry, though. We don't have to rely on your wings to find the portal."

I let my face ask the obvious.

"Me," Rohin says with a smile that screams Alex. "I'll just request asylum in your realm, and a gatekeeper is supposed to come talk to me."

My mother. Or my father. Or both could come and see a changeling requesting asylum.

"You know where the portal is? If you do, we can just go there now and see if I can open it. You do not even have to request asylum," I say.

"Not exactly," he explains, brushing past my comment but registering it with a confused expression. "'A clan may request admittance to the fae realm by a sincere plea in the area of a portal, making an offering of the fae tenets,' it says.

We don't *have* to be in front of the portal, just near it. We just need to wait for Tenneh and conjure up the offerings."

"What offerings?"

Tenneh materializes from among the trees, as a nymph would.

Rohin jumps, and my fists coat themselves in flames.

"You can't be startled if someone drops into your conversation when you're being loud about it," Tenneh says with no discernable attitude. "So, what offerings are you talking about?"

Rohin still takes a moment to catch his breath, so I jump in on his behalf.

"Our friend Rohin here," I say, pointing to Alex's latest form, "found a way to request asylum from the fae, thus having the portal come to us instead of us going to it."

Tenneh and I lock eyes. With the smallest of squints, I feel her push me to come forward with information that is not pertinent at this time.

"There is one small issue in that passage, Rohin," I continue, ignoring Tenneh's visual request. "It does not go with fae customs to request offerings. Are you sure that was the word used?"

"Pretty sure, yeah," Rohin says with a blank stare.

"Just read it again word by word," Tenneh adds with impatience.

"About that ...," Rohin begins, painting a mosaic of apologies in his face. "Your book got destroyed by the murdering fae I texted you about."

To everyone's surprise, even herself, I believe, Tenneh inhales deeply, closing her eyes, and exhales. She opens her eyes to find a blank expression on my face and the live artwork of guilt on Rohin's.

"If not offerings, what would your father deem acceptable representations of your values?" she asks.

It suddenly makes sense. The groups that have been granted asylum are, in fact, always groups. Not one being would be able to request it by themselves because only the fae are taught to exemplify all our values from birth. It's a clan request because the sum of all must be worthy enough of our values.

"Us … he would deem us acceptable representations," I say begrudgingly.

A dark magic wielder, possibly the last of the changelings, and the fae prince who crossed to the human realm for far too long. Half of me is thinking a plea from this group would never be strong enough to cross realms, yet the other half knows it is worth the try.

"Care to explain, Tinker Bell?" Rohin jumps in.

"Life, spirit, and balance," I explain. "Right now, none of us exemplifies all of them. I, myself, am not at peace with my spirit, as you said. Otherwise, my wings would be functional. But I am connected to life and nature.

"Tenneh, although a witch, you are the most assured being I have ever met. There is an unwavering sense of self and calmness that only comes from the connection a person has to their own spirit.

"And Rohin … Alex. You teeter between forms, never losing the basic principles that make you so uniquely yourself. Your actions, while incomprehensible to me, provide equilibrium to each other. No deed is a random act without another preceding it. The balance in yourself and your actions is exemplary of fae tenets."

The three of us, now standing, turn to look at each other. There is an unspoken reassurance among us. We are in this together. Our relationships may have started out of convenience and selfish intent, but I truly believe we have formed a bond that can cross realms.

"I guess you don't need this, then," Tenneh breaks the silence, holding up a small clear vial with golden dust.

"What is that?" Rohin and I ask in unison.

"Not much," she says. "I think I found a way to wake up your wings."

CHAPTER 30

Eva

As the sun is setting, Tenneh, Rohin, and I dive deeper into the woods, away from the marked paths.

To make way, I'm moving plants while Tenneh keeps chanting, "Quaeso ut de medio fiat," to achieve the same thing.

Once at a clearing among the woods, Tenneh extends her arms to her sides, closes her eyes, and says, "Nihil nos paulisper."

"What was that?" Rohin asks.

"Temporary protection from prying eyes," she explains.

Tenneh picks up a stick from the ground and begins drawing a circle around me. She pulls out a small disc from her cross bag and sticks her thumb in it. She leans forward to place her thumb on my forehead, and I meet her halfway by crouching.

"What is it?"

"Pulverized roses and other things," she says with the faintest smile.

I smile back, reassuring her I can take the truth of whatever it is she is using in her concoction.

"Robin's blood," she adds. "Don't worry. I did not kill it, and I let it fly free after giving it some food and water."

My smile turns brighter as Rohin's confused expression turns more complex.

Tenneh pulls out the vial with the golden dust again and sighs.

"What is that?" Rohin asks for me.

"This is Elior's crushed wing extract with … our dried blood."

Silence joins us in this clearing, and it takes the floor, if only for a moment.

"We all arrived at the same conclusion, albeit through different roads," Tenneh explains in a calming, almost soothing voice. "Elior's memory and wings were sort of glamoured to not be recognized by him and to block the memory of what happened to him. Our essences combined can lift the veil of the glamour … and the one you have on right now, by the way."

"My entire 'essence' is hiding from a mistake, and my abilities reflect the same," Rohin hangs his head and admits mostly to himself. "I don't see how a coward's blood can uncover any truths."

"Do you want some balloons?" Tenneh asks.

Perplexed at the question, Rohin and I can only stare back at her with blank expressions.

"For your pity party?" she adds. "You made choices, as we all have. But you also met someone in need, and you've done everything in your power to help a wingless butterfly safely return home. Also, your abilities are about visibility. So, that helps with the glamour in any way I will it to."

"She develops a sense of humor on my last night in this realm," I say as a joke, but it changes the tone to a somber one.

Tenneh continues making different markings on the ground and instructs Rohin to stay back and not touch any of the symbols.

"We only have one shot at this, so please do not interrupt me," she clarifies.

She clasps the vial with the dust between her palms and mutters a prayer to herself. She then proceeds to pour the entire contents of the vial in her left hand and begins to circle me while pouring the powder on me little by little.

"Excitare, quae dormit. Apparet qualis est occultatum. Illuminare his quae obscurabitur."

I close my eyes and try to concentrate on moving my wings as much as I can. I begin to feel a tingle in them and become acutely aware of every inch of skin being covered by them.

The area where wings meet skin begins to feel warmer and warmer, as Tenneh continues chanting her phrase. The warmth turns to a searing burn. I try to hold on as long as I can, thinking the pain would only be temporary. Still, when I hear Tenneh stumble on the words she has been flawlessly chanting for a while, I open my eyes to see hers widened and my wings glowing in red.

I begin to scream in pain while Tenneh continues circling and chanting. This is trial by fire, and my wings are being burned out of my body.

Seeing that Tenneh is only chanting louder through my screams, Rohin starts yelling at her to stop.

No one can hear one another, and Rohin charges in my

direction. As soon as he steps into the circle of markings Tenneh made on the floor, he is stopped in his tracks.

The three of us are frozen for a short moment, which gives enough time for each to lock eyes with the other.

The only thing going through my mind is that this is how I die today. So close to getting back home.

A blinding ring of red light shoots from my wings and knocks the three of us down.

When I come to my senses, I rush over to Tenneh, who is the closest to me, and see she's just gathering herself as well. We both then turn to Rohin, who is not there.

In the place of Rohin, there's a writhing, smaller, fair-skinned blonde girl with a scarred face.

"Alex?" Tenneh and I ask in unison.

The girl sits up and looks at her hands and begins touching herself as if to check to make sure she's all there.

In less time than it takes for anyone to blink, she changes back to Rohin.

I think we just saw Alex's original form.

"Elior!" Rohin says, pointing at me.

In a rush to check on them, I neglected my fully extended wings.

They're back. The pain from the process pales in comparison to the sense of feeling whole again.

"That was quite the show," a fourth voice says.

Before I can turn around, I watch as a net goes over Rohin—thrown by Lange.

I don't have to turn around to know that the owner of those words was Varya, which only means one thing: Eva is back.

I swirl up into the sky with matching elemental swords in my hands. My right has a flame short sword, while my left has turned the moisture around me into an ice spear.

Rohin is battling through the net. I take stock of the battlefield before making a move, and the usual suspects are there. Shoto, Lange, Varya, and Eva are surrounding the circle Tenneh drew on the ground.

Something is off.

They are not moving. Tenneh hasn't frozen them as she did to those men in the street before. They are … idling?

I come back down to the ground, weapons still in hand.

"Elior, I need to talk—," Eva begins, but I have already wielded vines to grab hold of her and her crew.

"You have no idea who you are dealing with," I tell the entire circle.

I spot Tenneh standing there, and I am relieved she did not suffer the same surprise attack Rohin did.

"Unfortunately," Tenneh says, "it's you who doesn't know."

Tenneh lifts both arms in the air and, with the same ease that she moves her limbs, the vines break.

My heart is struggling to comprehend what is going on, while my mind keeps screaming this was the expected outcome of working with a witch.

"Tenneh! Are you out of your mind?" Rohin screams from the net, earning himself a kick in the back from one of the goons.

"I'm not," she says. "This wasn't how we wanted things to go. But Rohin forced our hand."

I can't stand to see Alex being hurt and treated like a criminal.

"I'll give you ten seconds to explain yourself before I knock you all out," I say between gritted teeth.

My gauntlet is laid out.

"You'll do no such thing," Eva inserts herself in my conversation with Tenneh. "We—I just want to talk."

What pleasant chat is she expecting among friends who chase you, try to kill you, keep your friends trapped, and betray you?

I speak very slowly, so there is no confusion as to my request. "Let. Rohin. Go."

"Elior, dear, please listen. They won't hurt him if I don't say so. This is just insurance for you to talk to me."

Eva's brutal honesty is surprisingly persuasive. My options are limited for now.

"I do not want to see him on the ground, manhandled, or even touched by any of you."

"Of course," Eva agrees. "Lange, please help Mr. Rohin up and refrain from using force when not necessary."

"As you wish, boss," Lange responds in a mocking tone.

My eyes keep jumping among each person in this circle. When they land on Tenneh's, the once sculptured onyx-slated face is now riddled with anguish and doubt. Right now, she is the only real threat.

Eva waves Varya and Shoto away, and they walk over to Lange. Tenneh positions herself a few feet behind me, which makes me more nervous than being surrounded by Eva's goons, with their clearly visible lightning sticks poking out of their suit jackets.

"I see your wings are back," Eva says without breaking eye contact with me. "Tenneh really is an amazing witch."

I can feel my eyes roll involuntarily.

"Now that you are restored, of sorts," she continues, "do you not remember me?"

She wants to cross the portal. Why is she bothering with whether I remember her or not?

Eva looks past me to Tenneh, "You were able to fully unlock the charm?"

I look back as well and see Tenneh nod. "It might take some time before all the memories trickle in," the witch says.

"Well, we don't have that much time, with a full moon already gaining power, do we? How about something to jog your memory?"

So far, this conversation seems more of a monologue. I wonder if this is how she gets people to do what she wants. She's rather small to be physically intimidating. She must have a gift of gab to manipulate others.

"Get to the point," I tell her.

"That's very rude, Eli," she laughs.

My jaw drops, and I suddenly remember why I was jealous at the park when I saw her. We were once lovers.

She's the reason I was crossing realms.

My wings briefly flutter, unable to give me the advantage of feigned ignorance.

"Good," Eva says. "Nice to be on the same level again, babe."

A burst of information about Eva just became clear in my mind. The way she wrinkles her nose when she eats something she doesn't like. The way she laughs when she is only being polite, and the way she truly laughs when something is funny to her. The way she relies too much on the word "sure" for every situation.

Eva is a fully realized person in my mind. Someone I loved … love. Someone who does not match the person I have known the past few days. With my memories blocked or unblocked, I don't know this recent Eva.

"My love," I say habitually, hoping it will garner some goodwill with her. "What is going on? Why are these people here? Can you and I talk without them? I feel like this is the first time I am seeing you in a long time."

That last part is true. Unfortunately, I do not like what I see.

Eva smiles, and her expression softens. Her shoulders relax, and she switches to breathing only through her nose.

"Our plan is finally coming together, babe."

Her eyes begin to water.

"We can finally go home," Eva continues. "We just need you to find the portal, and we can make the plea as a clan, together."

Unsure if she overheard my discussion earlier with Tenneh and Rohin, I ask to confirm, "Who is *we*?"

Once again, Eva looks past me to Tenneh, who, in turn, does a clearing motion with both hands and washes away some of the shadows from the trees around us.

A group of about twenty fae-looking people comes forward—some with extended wings, others with no wings at all.

I can spot some of them holding up Farha, Rahim, and Priya.

PART III

CHAPTER 31

Trust

Tenneh is quiet. Her slight expressions that usually speak volumes for her have been muted. Rohin, who voices almost every thought that crosses his mind, has been muzzled by the sheer number of people surrounding us.

"Our plans got derailed before, but now we have strength in numbers," Eva says. "And weapons to aid our cause."

In a show of force and likely an intimidation tactic, all the people surrounding us, including Eva's goons, pull out small baton-like sticks and have them crackle lightning.

Seeing how uncomfortable it makes me, Eva raises her hand, motioning for everyone to power down their sticks.

"Just so I don't bore you with the details, what do you remember, my love? And what is still missing?"

"I only remember you," I respond. "Indulge me if you will."

She pulls out her phone from her back pocket to check something. She then looks up to the sky, directly at the rising moon.

"Sure, we have some time."

Eva circles me and takes stock of myself, Tenneh, the fae-looking group, Rohin, and her hired help.

"It was your idea, really," she began. "As you know, I grew up knowing about the fae and the creation of another realm. But as I learned of the fate of the changelings, I figured the realm had ceased to exist. Years later, I met you."

Eva turns to face me. Like a cat ready to pounce.

"Handsome, charming, and funny," she continues. "What more could I ask for? Then, I learned you had not only come from the fae realm, but you were its prince."

Gaps are starting to fill in. Scenes of meeting Eva for the first time in New York. Her teaching me about cars and technology.

"And we talked about the realm for many hours," I interject. "You asked me to take you there, and I said that as beautiful as you were, I could not take you there because you were human—"

"And that's when I said," she cuts me off now, "I was only part human, and that there was still a part of me that was fae."

The same feeling of disbelief I had the first time I heard this comes rushing back down on me. A sobering waterfall of knowledge reminds me of the spoils of the Great War.

Not all fae made it to Lempara in its birth. Some of them were too far away from the first portals. Others were traitors to the fae race itself.

In the silence between us, Rohin yells from his netted prison.

"What happened to the changelings?"

"He doesn't know?" Eva asks me, perplexed and excited.

"You've been with him for how long and you haven't told him?" she says to me. "This is amazing, and so unlike you! You've known this for years. I doubt the memory block wiped this little nugget out. Huh … I'm learning new things about you every day."

"There hasn't been a good time," Tenneh tries to salvage.

Anger and shame mix for a cocktail of hurt poured into my chest. Tenneh has no business inserting herself between Rohin and me after the stunt she is pulling with Eva.

I walk over to Rohin, and Varya steps in, pointing her lightning stick directly at my chest. I realize I am still holding my elemental weapons, so I subside them and raise my hands.

Looking directly at Rohin, I say, "I should have told you this sooner, but there is a reason I think you are the last of your kind.

"I believe it was a few human decades ago when the self-proclaimed last group of changelings requested asylum in Lempara. At the time, they claimed to be persecuted by other humans, something my father did not completely believe, given the strong connection between both races. So, he denied their request."

Rohin is staring blankly and waiting for the redeeming part of this story. I'm not sure what to say, so I keep adding context.

"There was also the fact that during the Great War, changelings aided the humans in the killing of our kind."

"So, you decided to return the favor?" Rohin finally says. "Tell me, does the extinction of an entire race abide by your tenets?"

There is no defense for my father's action. I can only stand there and take it with a hung head.

"I should have told you sooner. I am sorry."

"You've done a lot of apologizing lately for someone who's so clear on their beliefs," Rohin throws back.

The words are meant to be cutting, and they, in fact, feel like sharp knives stabbing my chest.

I turn around to walk back to Eva when I hear Rohin say, "Yeah, walk away, Tinker Bell."

My head lifts, but I hold the urge to look back. Instead, my eyes meet Tenneh's, who also caught Rohin's use of my moniker and raises her eyebrows ever so slightly.

Back facing Eva, I slump to sit on the ground.

"Join me, please," I say.

"Don't tell me you have feelings for a changeling, babe," she says mockingly, sitting on the ground across from me.

"Even if we open the portal," I say calmly, ignoring her remark. "What makes you think my father, or anyone in the realm for that matter, would allow part-humans to cross? You know what the decision was on the changelings."

"Because we have you on our side," Eva says.

Upset with the wordplay and preambles, Tenneh interrupts the conversation once more.

"Your realm is dying," Tenneh says flat out. "Lempara is tethered to the human realm, and the state of ours is making yours die little by little. If the fae don't begin cutting back on their constant expansion, further draining our polluted resources, both realms are going to cease."

Dread fills my body. Once again, the familiar feeling of disbelief washes over me, but it fills another memory gap.

Eva and I have had this conversation before. I know she is telling the truth.

And they need me specifically to be the ambassador for their request. They don't just want to go to Lempara, they want to leave the portals open, so energy can flow between realms, and be the last ones to establish themselves in the fae realm.

Not having Tenneh or Rohin to guide me, I follow my instincts.

"Let us open a portal then," I relent.

With my hands on the ground, I will it to trap Eva in what looks like a small volcano with her head at its peak.

The entire group and Eva's goons step forward to her defense. I extend both arms and gesture them to stop, and they follow suit.

"But I kindly ask that you release Rohin. I am going to need him for this, my love."

Eva smiles.

"Sure. Anything you need, babe."

The ground around her subsides. Eva gestures to Lange to release Rohin.

Once released, I run over to meet Rohin. He opens his eyes widely, asking me to stop before embracing.

Rohin extends his hand for me to shake, and, once I do, he pulls me closer in a half hug.

"OK, what's the plan?" he whispers in my ear.

"Making it up as I go along."

We are surrounded by prying eyes. Every action we take, every sentence we utter, is being watched and heard.

Hopefully, they didn't hear that last confession.

When I turn around to face Eva, I find that she is merely three steps from me now.

"I am going to need Tenneh as well."

Eva smirks back as if I just asked her to be a part of this herself.

"Tenneh is free to do as she pleases. She is not following anyone's orders but her own."

The fact that her words are meant to slight doesn't make it hurt any less.

"Tenneh, dear, would you mind assisting Prince Elior here in opening the portal to the fae realm?"

Stoic iciness returns to Tenneh's face.

"Don't call me dear."

Tenneh walks over to Rohin and me without saying another word.

"I guess I have to find the portal now," I admit to the group.

My wings start to flutter until they begin to faintly glow. The flutter turns to rhythmic flaps.

They know where to go.

I know where to go.

CHAPTER 32

Truth

After a failed attempt to fly ahead of the group and maybe have a private conversation with Rohin and Tenneh, I learn at least two others in the following group also have working wings.

We get to another wooded area after passing a larger lake. I have to wait until those walking catch up.

Lange and Shoto are keeping their weapons out and walking alongside Rohin, while Varya is keeping close to Eva. In any other circumstance, it would be curious to see Tenneh walking with a group in general, but the betrayal of your own comfort levels pales in comparison to the betrayal of a friend.

I land on the ground before me, with the two other half-faes following suit.

There's not much to see in this area of the park. For all intents and purposes, it looks about the same as the clearing we made down south, except here neither Tenneh nor I have to move any plant life to the side.

The moon is now beaming bright and full, directly down at us. I feel the energy in my wings. My entire body is feeling rooted to this place at this moment. I don't believe in destiny, but I know I'm supposed to be here right now.

"Rohin. Tenneh," I call upon a friend I hurt and a friend who hurt me.

My mind is racing with plausible scenarios. I can rain fire on everyone once Rohin is safely near me, but Tenneh could easily stop me at such close range. I can lift the ground we stand on to lift us out of there, but I risk hurting Rohin. Then, I realize that none of them have ever seen a portal, let alone how it opens.

Rohin gets to my side first, and we both watch as Tenneh slumps over.

I swear I see her mouth the word "please," and my anger toward her somewhat subsides. The closer she gets, the more I can see behind the icy glare. There's a melted sea of sadness and worry behind her eyes.

I grab Rohin's left hand with my right and extend the other for Tenneh to grab. Rohin follows suit. Once we all link hands, I immediately will a strong wind ring around us.

"What are you doing? They can still see us," Rohin says, squeezing my hand tighter.

"Sound travels through the air. They can't hear us now," Tenneh explains for me. "Clever."

"Great," says Rohin. "What the hell, Tenneh?"

"Please be more specific, I'm not sure how long we can keep up this charade."

"How long have you been working with them?" I ask.

"Since the day Eva came over and you two hid in the

bathroom," Tenneh explains. "She explained what she was trying to do, and it aligned with what I myself had been seeing as a strong possibility for the future."

"What are you getting out of this?" Rohin jumps in.

"Hopefully, a sustainable realm."

"It is not the fae's fault that humans have been so careless with their own realm. Why should we have to pay the price for your kind's mistakes?"

"I don't know your highness. We didn't tether the realms, the fae did. But you either open the portal or these people will kill Alex. They are not playing around."

I try to think of what the next move is, but nothing comes to me. My mind is swirling as fast as the wind surrounding us, and it's just blurring any coherent thought.

Our hands are still linked. I take a deep breath and close my eyes, concentrating on Tenneh.

She's scared. About for herself, Alex, me ... everyone.

Concentrating on Rohin, I find the exact same feelings. I have no choice.

"Let us do this."

I calm the wind and lift the ground around slightly to get a vantage point of the group surrounding us, just in case.

Peeking over to the group, I see Eva's face is struggling between anger and aloofness. I remember she doesn't like to let people down. It's endearing, and it must be hard for her to have called upon this large group and place all their hopes in a reluctant player.

"Rohin, would you do the honors?" I ask him, with the most reassuring smile I can muster.

He takes a breath and closes his eyes.

"Dear Lempara, fae, gods, and kings," he stutters in what sounds like a question composed of an assortment of words he has heard regarding the fae realm.

I laugh to myself and reassure him, "Just make a sincere plea for your clan."

"OK," he says, and, with another breath, he begins again. "To Lempara's king and populace. We stand before you as the last remaining member of a race you neglected to protect, a member of a group who has helped to destroy your kind, and one of your own who has seemingly betrayed your beliefs. But we stand before you in unity, as a clan, exemplifying your tenets. Not a perfect one, mind you, but one that is able to recognize the strengths and faults within each other. A clan that can grow and learn, given whatever circumstance the world throws at it. A clan that does not judge its members but tries to learn from each other's mistakes.

"We do not request asylum. We request an audience with those in charge of the portal. And we ask that in the spirit of this clan's portrayal of your beliefs, you follow our tenets of openness, acceptance, and change."

Silence enters the group. Within its shroud, panic and anger slowly begin to wreak havoc.

I'm no expert with the asylum process, but I'm pretty sure you are disqualified if you say you are not requesting it.

My thoughts might as well have been yelled because Eva, followed by Varya, hastily came to us.

"Elior, my love," Eva begins in a rushed tone, and I feel Rohin grip my hand tighter in anger. "This was a valiant first attempt, but I think there's an opportunity here for you to actually lead your people."

She means the hybrids. My hands are still holding Tenneh and Rohin. I grab on tight to both of them, looking for counsel in front of Eva.

Anger and fear is coming from Rohin. Tenneh is brimming with disgust and … hope.

Eva's right. How can I hope to lead a realm created as a haven that has turned its back on the children of our own?

"I will try something else," I tell her, to buy myself some time. I'm still not clear on how to open a portal.

"I used to think you were being diplomatic with your answers, but I learned that you're just noncommittal when what you really want to do is say no," Eva says.

She's wrong. While that is true about me, in this case, I genuinely don't know what to do.

Eva turns to Rohin, looking to raise anger out of someone after her failed attempt with me. "Tell me, changeling, did he try to kiss you at a very inappropriate moment?"

Rohin's hand releases mine. His silence is accompanied by a pale face of admission.

"I thought so. Memories or not, you can't change who someone is at their core—an entitled brat."

Eva turns to Tenneh now, "Tenneh, beautiful Tenneh, do you think he trusts you?"

"Given that I lied to him. No, not anymore," Tenneh says, letting go of my hand.

"He never did. You were always a tool to him. That's why it's so easy for him to hold your hand right now and pretend you are a 'clan' together."

Eva turns back to Rohin, "This attempt didn't work, not because of you, sweetheart. It didn't work because this handsome prince does not really consider you a 'clan.' You two were always a means to an end. Did he even invite you to join him at Lempara? No? Didn't think so."

My eyes are fixated on Eva. Nothing else is within my focus. She is placing all her weight on her left leg. I bump some ground to push on her right foot, causing her to lose balance and fall forward to the ground. Once on the floor, both hands and feet are locked by rock mounds.

My ice spear in hand once more is being maneuvered entirely by rage and emotion.

As soon as I lift my weapon, a shock of lightning pierces my chest.

Varya is smirking.

Tenneh and Rohin do nothing, as I'm being immobilized. The group surrounding us is staring, almost pleased to see me hurt.

Now on my knees shaking, I see Shoto come forward and break Eva out of the rock shackles.

No one cares that I'm in pain. They see me agonize, and they're not putting a stop to it. I would be filled with righteous anger that these subjects are not protecting their prince, but the anger and hurt from the lightning stick doesn't compare to the hurt of seeing Rohin not even flinch.

He is standing there just talking to Tenneh through all of it, probably enjoying the karmic view of me being used as a key to prosperity like I promised them.

Finally, after a couple more hits to the face from Varya, Eva steps in. She played the part of the hero well. She pretended to be hurt and stall for time while Varya hit me, then rushed to save me from the consequences of the outburst she provoked.

"Are you OK, babe?" Eva asks in a high-pitched tone, crouched next to me with her hands on my shoulders. "Varya, please get away from here. How could you do such a thing? Elior didn't mean to hurt me. Look at him, he's bleeding."

That explains the taste of copper in my mouth.

Eva gets up and walks over to Lange and grabs a handkerchief from him.

Before Eva reaches me again, Tenneh comes from behind me and smears the blood from my mouth into her hand. I'm too weak to turn around, but I hear a cracking sound, and I see Eva's face misconfigured with rage.

"Now!" Rohin screams behind me.

As every single person in the group starts running toward Tenneh, Rohin, and I, they all seem to pause and suspend themselves mid-movement.

That's when I hear the continuous chant. "Genitor mihi dant parumper expande pallium."

I collapse to the ground and manage to roll my body over to look behind me. Tenneh is in a defensive stance, with her hands extended to her side, chanting without stopping.

Rohin comes over to me and kneels down.

"Still mad at you, Tinker Bell," he says with that familiar Alex smile. "But we're going to get you out of this."

He lifts my torso and drags me by the shoulders closer to Tenneh. A rush of adrenaline is wasted in my beat-up body and a lack of knowledge of what is happening.

Tenneh seems to have suspended everyone around us. Looking up from the ground at her, she's trembling but focused. She's even breaking a sweat.

Past her, in the sky, I notice a small bird is also suspended in the sky. Tenneh doesn't suspend the people around us. She suspends time itself.

Rohin reaches into Tenneh's bag and pulls two different vials with scarlet liquid in both. Blood.

He takes his shirt off, and, in the midst of all the silent commotion, I can't help but notice his muscular chest and how low his shorts are hanging off his pelvis.

Rohin uses his shirt to wipe my blood off of Tenneh's hand, proceeds to throw the shirt on the ground, and empties both blood vials on it.

With his right hand on Tenneh's back and his left holding up the blood-soaked shirt, he screams at me to grab his leg.

Once I manage to follow his instructions, he holds the shirt up and yells, through Tenneh's chant, "We seek asylum!"

I keep holding on for dear life.

"I would say sorry for letting you get your ass kicked, but I needed a second to tell Tenneh the rest of what that book said," Rohin explains. "Also, you kind of deserved it a little."

He looks down at me apologetically with a sweet smile. He's right.

All I can hear is Tenneh's chanting, which sometimes loses its rhythm.

Then, a bright golden fire illuminates the field.

This is it. The moment I've been waiting for. And whoever is on the other side of that portal will be sure to welcome the three of us to Lempara.

Light and chanting. That's all I remember.

In the blink of an eye, I am healed and on the other side of the portal facing my father—Melchoir, king of the fae realm Lempara.

CHAPTER 33

Lempara

It is disconcerting and almost violating to feel like someone took control of your body. Without a moment's notice, I am facing my father and my mother in front of me. Behind me, I can still see Rohin, Tenneh, and the entire scene at the park suspended in time.

But time works differently in Lempara. That scene could be happening slower or faster in the human realm than my breathing is happening here.

"It is good to see you, my son," my mother, Iris, says.

We're standing in a sunlit grass field, similar to the one we passed in the human realm to get to the clearing where the portal is. It goes well with my mother's white linen dress that displays intricacy in its embroidery but does not flaunt wealth in volume or jewels. A couple of trees in the distance are rustling from the light breeze, and, by the position of the sun, it seems to be about midday.

This is quite a welcoming stage for asylum seekers. Nice enough to crave entrance, but without any discernible qualities for petitioners to recognize if not accepted. The field is spacious enough for large groups but also manageable to make it just tight enough if the spacing-excuse rejection were to be needed.

Seeing this place for the first time makes me think differently about the asylum missions.

"Did you look for me?" I ask.

Greetings and pleasantries, take a step back to the question that has been lingering in my mind since I woke up in a park.

"You remember that night?" she replies.

Her slim angular face transfixes with surprise. She takes a step back, leaving the floor open for my father to speak.

The truth is, since my memories were unblocked, I haven't had time to think of the specifics of that night. Bits and pieces come back to me. Mainly, my father pointing the staff he is holding to his side straight at my face.

"Some of it. It is slowly coming back to me," I admit. "Why were you pointing your staff at me, dad?"

He has not moved a muscle since I came to be in front of him. His green eyes fixate on mine.

"Who cut your hair?" he deflects my question with another, his own pink hair blowing in the breeze.

Taken aback by his question, I run my hands through my hair and remember Alex cut my hair in a gymnasium locker room.

"A changeling did," I look at him and say proudly. "The same one who conjured the portal to bring me back here. The same one who …"

Drip by drip, a basin of recollections begins to fill my mind.

"... the same one who protected and helped me after you attacked me."

It takes everything in me not to crumble and to hold back my tears. Not this time. This time my tears will not be a distraction for people to not take me seriously or not answer for their actions.

My father turns to my mother, who, in turn, looks at me with a disappointed look on her face.

It's unclear whether the disappointment is with my father, or with me for calling out my father.

"Are you hurt?" he asks.

"No."

"Did you wake up surrounded by nature?"

"Yes."

"In the realm, you so desperately wanted to be in?"

Drip, drip.

I do remember fighting with him about being in the human realm that night he blasted me.

"Why did you—"

"I am speaking," he says, loudly and commandingly. "You, of all people, should know how hard this was for me. But in the end, I chose to give you what you wanted. Your life, your love, your freedom, your realm.

"I am your father. But I am a father to this realm, first. And I was not about to endanger Lempara by letting you open our borders to the humans."

For a man who prides himself in his own balance, seeing him portray any sort of strong emotion is rare.

Drip, drip.

My mother, noting his temper, walks over and

places herself between us. Somewhat relieved that she is de-escalating the situation, I let down my guard and begin to feel the lingering effects of being repeatedly struck with lightning blows.

"It truly is great to see you again, my son. But the request of asylum is not to be played with," she says. "And I must ask, how did you even know to come back to Lempara this way?"

They were never looking for me. She's surprised and disappointed I'm here.

Drip, drip.

"That same changeling helped me, with the aid of a witch," I say, and realize that it wasn't just them. "And Eva."

I'm not really sure which part of that sentence was most egregious to them. But we've had this conversation before. A similar one, at least. About Eva's plan—our plan.

"You already know the human realm is dying, do you not?" I ask. The question is not meant for anyone to answer, but for my thought to materialize in the world and be real. "We have been in this same place before. And you chose to cast me out. You attacked your own son and blocked my memories of how to get back, so you would not have to deal with the reality that we *need* humans."

"To be young and foolish, my dear," my mother says. "Our realms are tethered, that much is true, but we need not worry about the human realm. As it can be easily—"

"Tinker Bell," Rohin interrupts, poking his head and torso through the portal. "Are you good? This is the right realm, right? Listen, Tenneh is getting tired, but we just wanted to make sure you made it home all right."

I can faintly hear Tenneh's continuous chant in the background. Rohin's smile is beaming at me, paired with sadness in his eyes.

Drip, drip.

"Tell Tenneh to stop and bring everyone here," I tell him.

"You will do no such thing, changeling," my father roars, pointing his staff at Rohin and bringing him closer.

Rohin writhes. Having his body moved by another being is violating. Appalled by my father's action, I take a stronger stance and raise a wall of rock between my father and Rohin. My mother quickly counters and trips me with vines on the ground, without even flinching.

"Why are you doing this?" The situation is ridiculous, and everyone involved is acting out of character.

The wall I raised falls back down and my father's punch catches Rohin's face by surprise, knocking him straight to the ground to meet the rubble of my wall.

"I am sorry, son," my father says. "But I cannot let you endanger this realm. I will ask you, once again, leave and do not attempt to come back."

Drip, drip.

The basin is full.

"Eva wants to merge the realms, which would take you out of power. That is why you do not want more portals? Lempara will die if you do not merge!"

"No!" he roars. The once laidback smiling father who taught me how to fly faster and control the energy in nature is now red in the face, screaming at his firstborn son. "I will seal all the portals, and the humans will die."

"The realm will outlast them," my mother jumps in,

with no intent of defusing the situation. "We made sure of it would a long time ago. The humans had every opportunity for balance, and now they must reap the consequences of their actions toward nature. Try to kill nature, and it will kill you back. A simple trade."

I've heard this before, and I become mad at myself all over again for not remembering sooner.

"They are fighting for their lives," I say, pointing to the portal.

"They are not," my father says with calm disdain. "They are looking for another saving grace. Another temporary fix to the problems of their own creation."

"True as that may be, we cannot let them die!"

"Do you forget that their kind tried to kill ours?" my mother is quick to retaliate. "I expect better from you."

"Not all of them … and not all our kind were keen on having a separate realm, were they? Otherwise, who are those on the other side? How are Eva and her group here? How are a changeling and a witch helping a fae cross the portal by himself?

"You are wrong about humans. They may have their faults, but at least they do not try to pretend to live by some tenets they discard at convenience. Life, spirit, and balance. Nice way of keeping everyone in line."

My father grabs his staff horizontally with both hands. His wings begin to glow a soft gold. My mother, buying him time, is trying to trap my feet with rock shackles. I take up to the air, and so does she.

She tries to move the air beneath my wings to make me fall, but I will it back to its place. We're in a wind battle, moving air and drafting gusts at each other. Both wanting to knock the other out without causing any real harm. My instinct would be to strike my opponent, but I can't do that to my mom. I let her move the wind beneath me, and I fall to the ground.

As I'm falling, I see my father ready to beam that golden light at me once more. Something he must have learned from dark magic wielders, I'm now realizing. Inches before I hit the ground, I open the earth beneath me and bury myself in it. With limited air, my plan better work.

I dig my hands deep in the earth and close my eyes to concentrate. I remember Tenneh's advice to calm myself and listen.

I hear my mother's feet touch the ground. Running out of air myself, I will the roots deep within the soil to rise up and immobilize her entire body.

When I rise from the ground and come up for air, I'm able to see my mother detained on the ground with thick roots holding her down at every joint. I'm entirely covered in dirt myself when I realize that my father is glowing in gold.

Melchoir, the king of Lempara, has his foot on Rohin's unconscious chest, pointing his staff at his head while staring at his own son.

"What do you want?" I scream at him.

"For you to leave and not try to come back," he says. And to my surprise, I see tears roll down his face.

His face turns from despair to anger once more. I realize his glare is directed behind me. I look back, and Tenneh is standing with Eva.

"I couldn't hold the chant for too long, and when neither

the portal closed nor Rohin came back, I knew there was something wrong," Tenneh explains, trying to justify her setting foot in the fae realm.

As much as my father's blood is boiling to have a dark magic wielder in his land, Tenneh's is probably doing the same for being there.

He lifts his staff and swings it around, making all of us duck for cover, but he aims it at my mother and releases her from my shackles.

"King Melchoir and Queen Iris, I—," Eva begins. But before she can continue, my parents move in unison to blast Tenneh, Eva, and myself across the portal.

The three of us land on our backs in the field at Central Park.

In what seems like a déjà vu moment for me, I see my father step across the portal. It would be a momentous occasion that could symbolize peace between the realms if he and my mother weren't on the warpath to close the portal they just crossed.

My dad is hovering over the ground, holding Rohin by the neck.

He's going to kill Rohin if he doesn't let him go soon.

"Stop this!" I yell at them.

My scream is ignored by my parents and the twenty other people on the field. Seeing Eva and Tenneh knocked to the field and struggling to stand, prompts Varya and her goons to launch an attack, followed by the fae hybrids.

One by one, my mother strikes them without flinching. A winged hybrid comes from above, and she handles it by blowing a precise straight flame upward, burning a hole through his right wing.

Another hybrid girl runs zigzagged toward my mom and slides on the ground below her. She almost strikes my mom with the lightning stick, but before her hand reaches up, the queen of fae makes two fists in the air, causing tree roots to pin the hybrid girl to the ground.

Lange surprises her from the back and headlocks my mother, bringing her to the ground. Holding her neck with his right arm, he swings his left arm to slam the stick onto her chest.

"No!" I scream instinctively and stomp my foot on the ground to raise a small boulder and extend my fist to send it straight to his head.

It's a clean hit, and my mother breaks free.

"Which side are you on?" Eva protests.

"My own."

Only Tenneh, Eva, Varya, Lange, and Shoto are left standing.

Rohin's neck is still under my father's grip. His body is limp, and my worst fears begin to materialize.

"Let him go," Tenneh orders for herself and me.

My father smirks and turns to me.

"This is what happens when you talk to these things, son. They suddenly think they can address the fae, and even make demands."

Tenneh narrows her eyes and begins to mutter words I can't make out.

Before she can finish, my father aims his staff at her and creates a small air twister around her head.

He's asphyxiating her.

I take a stance to help Tenneh, but my mother pulls the same trick I did to her and immobilizes me against a tree.

"No!" I scream.

While my mother's preoccupied with Tenneh and me, Eva runs straight at her blind spot, with a lightning stick in hand. She must have figured that they can't be reasoned with, and in my parents' absence, I would inherit the throne and his staff.

My father sees this and turns his attention to Eva, releasing Tenneh from his twister, who falls on the ground.

Eva was expecting this. She throws the lightning stick up in the air as my dad turns the ground beneath her to mud and traps her legs. Varya then appears from the shadows behind Eva and jumps to slam the stick in the air toward my mom and throw her own at my father at the same time.

Both sticks land on their intended targets, electrifying them for a second. They're going for the kill and have the perfect self-defense excuse.

My father finally releases Rohin. Before the king of fae is able to reach out and grab him again, Rohin turns into a full black jaguar in a matter of seconds and bites my father's hand.

Blood is falling on the field, and my dad drops his staff—the only tool he has to permanently close a portal.

Shoto grabs it and runs toward Eva. My mother, having regained her balance, flies straight at him with a flame sword in her right hand.

It's a direct hit.

I just witnessed my mother kill a human.

Varya takes her opening, picks up Eva's lightning stick, and runs to hit my mother on the back with it.

Unable to intervene, I can do nothing but scream at the horrors I'm witnessing.

The few hybrids in the group who are conscious or regaining consciousness begin to flee at the sight of looming death.

Lange jumps in between the women, grabs the staff, and runs it over to Eva.

My father is finally able to fire whip Alex off his arm, and turns his attention to Lange, Varya, Eva, and my mom.

Taking it as a breather, Alex goes over to check on Tenneh, who's still regaining her composure.

Seeing my mother on the ground, with Varya standing over her, makes my father yell at the top of his lungs. The ground cracks underneath Varya, essentially burying her up to her waist. He is flying straight toward her, but Eva stands over Varya with my father's staff pointing directly at him.

He stops in his tracks.

To everyone's surprise, the only two words out of her mouth are, "Release him." She looks at me without lowering the staff.

"Insolent half-breed. As if you could ever know how to wield a king's staff," he snarks at Eva.

"Then why'd you stop charging?" Eva snaps back. She moves the staff with her arms, expecting something to happen. But I know from experience that if she is not manipulating energy in nature, the staff won't serve her any purpose.

The staff only acts as a magnifier of fae abilities. In the

hands of those with no energy abilities, it's just a wooden stick.

My father smirks and continues to charge, but Eva changes her hand placement on the staff and bats my father on the head. A move no one was expecting.

Eva then looks over to Tenneh and the jaguar and throws the staff their way. Tenneh grabs it.

Enraged, Melchoir is spewing golden flames from his mouth, hands, and feet.

Tenneh roars the words, "Corpus quod in aqua in aqua ut control." And, before the king of fae can make any moves, the Caribbean witch brings him to his knees.

"Eva, dig out Varya," Tenneh barks. "Alex, help Elior down. Quickly!"

Alex changes to his Brett form, I assume, because it's her strongest physical form.

Tenneh continues to hold my father, as Brett and Eva dig their respective companions out of their traps.

I glance at both of them digging, sweating, and desperately trying to save them from certain death. The past actions of the rescuer don't matter right now. All that matters are life and death, and whether this moment in time is anyone's to choose the fate of another.

As soon as I land on solid ground, I thank Brett by kissing his lips briefly, before running to Tenneh.

She motions me to stand next to her and passes the staff to me.

"There was a life you led, and there is a life you created for yourself. It's up to you to decide who you want to be going forward. No one person or circumstance can make that choice for you," Tenneh says.

I look closer at her and see a flood of tears flowing down her onyx demeanor.

I take this cue to hold my father in the same manner I previously held Eva.

Tenneh releases her enchantment on Melchoir and is dizzied by the amount of energy she divested. The staff can do that to inexperienced users.

Brett is there to hold her up.

"So, what now, son? You are going to let humans, half-breeds, changelings, and dark magic wielders into our realm?" my dad spits at me. "I hope you are ready to see Lempara and its people, your own family, die."

The words hit me worse than any blow of lightning.

"You were so ready to eliminate me before, and today ..."

"You made that choice for yourself! Your mother and I gave you exactly what you wanted."

"I wanted convergence. For life to flourish and for you to accept Eva and me."

The notion is correct, but the words feel foreign—a love that feels just as real as the one I have for Alex and like a distant dream at the same time.

"What you want is of no concern to a king. What you needed is what you got from me."

I look over to Eva, and Lange is helping Varya climb out of the ground.

"Eva, please bring my mother, Queen Iris, here," I ask, and she obliges.

Once the king and his unconscious queen are together, I raise the staff and point it at them.

"Elior!" Eva says in horror.

Looking around me, I find that Brett, Tenneh, Varya, and Lange all share the same expression.

I smirk and think out loud.

"I am not my father's son. Not anymore. I am not a traitor to my kin or my kind. And I am not a traitor to the fae tenets. Life, spirit, and balance—but as I see them."

A golden hue envelops my wings and the staff in my hands. Slowly but surely, a new portal opens behind my parents.

My father laughs mockingly.

As soon as I start to see some light on the other side of the small portal, the golden hue becomes less intense, and my arms start shaking.

Without a word, Eva, Brett, and Tenneh help me steady the staff, and the portal resumes to open.

In shock, my father starts crying and screaming for my mother to wake up.

With my own tears streaming down my face, I tell them, "I love you more than words can describe, and I owe almost all of who I am to you both. Please, care for each other and for Lempara."

The portal, now stable enough to remain open, shows a small forest I recognize as the one behind our castle grounds.

No more words are exchanged, as I move my mother and my father across the portal—and close it.

CHAPTER 34

Aftermath

After closing the second portal, the living who remain rest in the darkness of the night.

Only the faint glow of the moonlight guides us in helping the unconscious up.

Brett enlarges his arms to carry people and line them up. Tenneh is muttering some healing spell on each one, and Eva makes sure they are well enough to make it back to their homes.

None of us have spoken about what happened a few minutes ago. I think we're all still trying to process it.

I hear coughing from the corner where Tenneh is tending to the fae hybrids. When the coughing continues for a few minutes, I go over to see what's happening.

To my surprise, I recognize Farha as the fae who's struggling.

"Something's blocking her airway," Tenneh says when I get to her side, without taking her eyes from Farha. "I tried listening to her body, but I'm not sure it's her body causing this."

Following Tenneh's lead, I grab Farha's hand and close my eyes. I may not be able to sense her body like Tenneh can, but maybe I can see something else.

Alas, the blockage is dirt and water. She must've been screaming when my mother hit her with both elements straight on.

Under normal circumstances, I wouldn't dare try to move the elements from her airway. That would require surgical precision on elements you can't even see. But having the staff as a stronger connection emboldens me to try.

Holding Farha's hand with my right and the staff in my left, I close my eyes and let both guide me. In a matter of seconds, mud is lifted from Farha's open mouth.

She's somewhat drowsy, and Brett comes in to help her over to Eva.

"So, you're the king now?" Tenneh asks in her usual unemotive tone, without looking at me.

"Not really," I admit to her. "He can have another king's staff made if that is what you mean."

Silence falls between us again. As the remaining fae scatter, only Tenneh, Brett, Eva, and myself are left.

"What does the upside-down ten of cups mean?" I ask Tenneh to break the tension.

She looks straight into my eyes and says, "Violence."

I think Ms. Jessica doesn't give herself enough credit.

"Where did the murdering lady go?" I ask Eva of Varya.

"I believe you threw her back to her realm before you closed the portals," Eva answers.

An unnecessary but deserved slight, on both ends.

"If you're talking about Varya, I don't know what you mean by murdering," she says.

"She killed Ms. Jessica, the seer," I retort, indignant that her death didn't register in Eva's mind.

She furrows her brow then smiles, "Jesus Christ, we didn't kill her. We just sedated her."

At my disbelief, her expression changes to apologetic.

"I'm sorry," she says. "Varya, if that's her real name, and Lange left to take care of Shoto. She was aware of the risks and was expecting a larger payoff, so I'm sure she'll be back."

"What was she expecting?" Brett jumps in to ask.

"She wanted to make a new life in Lempara," Eva says, to the surprise of Brett and me.

I glance over to Tenneh, who's standing with her arms crossed and uninterested in the conversation.

"You knew all this," I accuse more than ask. "Why did you not tell me?"

Without changing her tone, position, or attitude, Tenneh simply says, "Because I didn't like you."

The deafening silence is broken by Brett's laughter. Subsequently, Tenneh smiles, followed by myself.

"It's true, though," Tenneh explains. "I did not trust you. You also have a grating personality when you first meet people. But when Eva here came to talk to me, she explained the situation with the realms.

"I knew something wrong was happening with the world. I knew nature was rebelling and something needed to be done. So, I signed on to her cause. She seemed smarter than you, with a clear plan, and all she asked of me was to help you find the portal."

My ego is bruised. More than anything, I pride myself on being charismatic and nice.

"The fact that they knocked out your colleague didn't raise any flags for you?" Brett asks, referring to Ms. Jessica.

"It did," Tenneh simply says. "But the morality of the question was whether one small act was going to stop me from helping ensure the continuation of this world."

"That makes no sense, Tenneh, and you know it. That small act speaks to what they were capable of," Brett protests.

"It's the trolley problem," Eva jumps in to explain, only to find a perplexed expression on my face. "Imagine there's a trolley, a train on a track headed to run over five people, but there's a lever you can pull to divert the train to another track that would only run over one person. What do you do? Do you do nothing, and five people die? Or do you actively choose to kill one to save five?"

"I chose to look the other way in the interest of an entire world. I could not hold Eva responsible for Varya's actions," Tenneh says in the plainest and clearest way possible.

I look over at Brett and can't help but feel foolish.

"I am so sorry for not being open to listening to you when I needed to be."

He smiles that damned smile from ear to ear and walks toward me.

In front of me, towering, imposing, making me feel protected, he says, "That's all I needed."

Brett leans forward and reaches my lips with his, making me forget the events of the entire night. For this moment, Alex and I are one, and I can't imagine anything better.

"Gross," Tenneh says, bringing us back to reality.

I smile at her and then reality hits me over the head once again.

Eva.

"What's your grand plan?" she says, with pain in her voice. "Put this all behind you and forget it ever happened … forget *we* ever happened?"

The words are meant to guilt me into something. I'm not sure what she expects, but her conviction doesn't make it clear either.

She is playing the part of the jealous ex-lover worse than she did the lover. And perhaps that is because she did love me. A notion now obscured by lies and lost in time.

"It is time to open more portals," I say, looking at the staff in my hand. "Without worrying about what is walking in or out of any realm. Lempara has placed a strain on the human realm, and it is time we open release valves."

"That won't help with the fact that the realm is dying," Eva condescendingly points out.

"I know," I respond. "But you heard my mother. The fae established precautions for nature to protect itself in a case like this. So, I am hoping I can count on the best witch I know, and the last of the changelings, to help me turn things around."

I look over to Tenneh and Brett, making my best attempt to plead with my eyes. But I can see the hesitation in both of them.

"Tenneh," I prod. "You said you *did* not like me. Does that mean you do now?"

"Tolerate, at best."

The corner of her mouth is tugged from one side, telling me not all hope is lost.

"Brett." I turn my attention to the most wonderful being across the realms. "I know you had your own plan before I completely ruined it, with no gold to show for it … yet. But I am offering a mission where we could help entire civilizations and realms. I understand your path may take you elsewhere, and I am not the easiest person to deal with. But I think there is something to be said of our teamwork."

"Your people let mine die," Brett says simply. "Yes, I have no emotional connection to any other changeling, but I was never given the opportunity."

He pauses, and so does my heart.

"I don't want that to happen to any other living being," he finally says with a smile. "How can I trust that you won't sell me out when times get tough, Tinker Bell? It seems the fae have a habit of doing that."

"We are all living in the same universe, where the wind blows, waves crash, embers flare, and the planet turns. But I will give my life, I don't care what it costs, because I love you until the end of the realms."

"This is what I have to look forward to?" Tenneh asks. "I'd rather go back to working with Eva."

The moon is still glimmering in that brief moment when she shares the sky with the sun every day.

Dejected, Eva begins to walk away.

"Eva," I cry after her. "Can we walk you to wherever you're going?"

CHAPTER 35

Goodbye

Walking shirtless with my wings contracted—by choice, this time—feels daring and new.

Brett changes to Alana's form. Tenneh uses some powders and mixes to brighten her appearance. She then proceeds to apply the same on my face because I am, as she says, "wrecked."

It's oddly silent to walk someone to the underground wagons who just hours ago was fine with seeing you dead. But Eva was doing what was best for herself and her people. I can understand that.

"Do you want me to open a portal near you?" I make the offer to break the ice.

Eva looks puzzled and relieved at the same time.

"No," she says. "Just figure out how to open as many as you can, and let me know if one is close. I'm not advising any in my group to cross realms, but I want to give them the option."

"Will do."

We get to the dirty set of stairs that lead to lower levels.

I will never get used to the fact that humans move as moles do underground.

Eva extends her hand to Tenneh, who meets it halfway.

"I'll keep you abreast of the portals," Tenneh offers as one last token.

"Thank you," Eva responds, then turns her attention to Alana. "Take care of him, please."

Alana, brow furrowed, offers no response.

Eva looks at me and opens both arms, asking for a hug. I oblige and see from the corner of my eye that Alana rolls hers.

With no words of goodbye, I give a half-hearted smile to one of the most complicated people I have ever loved.

She turns to leave, and I remember something.

"Eva, wait—if getting to Lempara was your plan all along, how did you find me in the first place?"

Eva smiles, turns around, and places her left hand on my right cheek. "That's a story for another time, my love."

"What will you do now?" I ask.

"Meet my boyfriend. And then, I have to go see about some girls in the South causing trouble."

And, as swiftly as she came into my life, she leaves.

Tenneh, Alex, and I watch hand in hand as Eva goes down the stairs and disappears. I'm feeling a sense of relief, sadness, anger, and anxiety, manifested in one tear I hide from Alana.

"Can we go get breakfast?" Alana asks.

"Sure," Tenneh responds. "I'd love to know what happened to my aunt's book."